D1218934

THE TROUBLE KID

Center Point
Large Print

Also by Wayne D. Overholser and available from Center Point Large Print:

Twin Rocks
Black Mike
The Durango Stage
Proud Journey

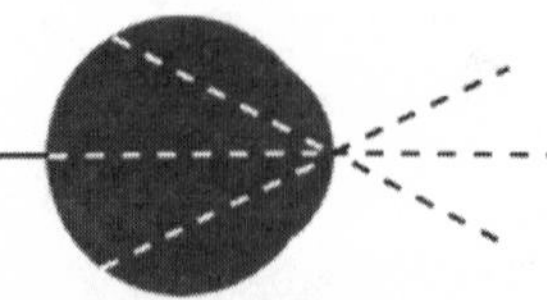

This Large Print Book carries the Seal of Approval of N.A.V.H.

THE TROUBLE KID

WAYNE D. OVERHOLSER

CENTER POINT LARGE PRINT
THORNDIKE, MAINE

This Center Point Large Print edition
is published in the year 2016 by arrangement with
Golden West Literary Agency.

First US edition: Ace Books
First UK edition: Gunsmoke

The text of this Large Print edition is unabridged.
In other aspects, this book may vary
from the original edition.
Printed in the United States of America
on permanent paper.
Set in 16-point Times New Roman type.

ISBN: 978-1-62899-943-3 (hardcover)
ISBN: 978-1-62899-947-1 (paperback)

Library of Congress Cataloging-in-Publication Data

Names: Overholser, Wayne D., 1906–1996, author.
Title: The trouble kid / Wayne D. Overholser.
Description: Center Point Large Print edition. | Thorndike, Maine : Center Point Large Print, 2016. | ©1978
Identifiers: LCCN 2016003669| ISBN 9781628999433 (hardcover : alk. paper) | ISBN 9781628999471 (pbk. : alk. paper)
Subjects: LCSH: Large type books. | GSAFD: Western stories.
Classification: LCC PS3529.V33 T764 2016 | DDC 813/.54—dc23
LC record available at http://lccn.loc.gov/2016003669

CHAPTER I

I hadn't been at my desk for more than five minutes when the Big Man sent for me. His name was Roscoe Gentry, but he was always called the Big Man behind his back, though I'm sure he knew about his nickname and I have a hunch he liked it. His word was law around the *Rocky Mountain News* office, and no one who valued his job argued with him about anything if he wanted to keep said job.

My name is Curt Curran, and I liked what I was doing. I suppose you'd call me a roving reporter. If there was an assignment that smacked of danger and called for an investigation, I was the one who got tapped; but this time I was close to rebellion. I'd just got in on the train from Casper, and I'd come directly to the newspaper office. I should have gone home, and now I wished to hell I had.

The rebellion didn't last long. About ten seconds, I guess. Long enough for me to remind myself that this was the best job I'd ever had and I wasn't likely to get another one like it. I didn't have a wife or any close kin, so I was free to go anywhere or do anything. I got up and went into the Big Man's office. He was reading a news story and didn't look up or pay the slightest attention to me. I knew that was his way, so I sat down and waited.

He finished the last page and laid it down, then picked up a cold cigar and lit it. He said, "I was reading your last story. It just came in. I gather that you wrote it and mailed it in Casper."

I nodded. "That's right. I didn't figure I had time in Buffalo."

"A good job," he said. "Was it really as touchy as you say? I mean, you didn't exaggerate?"

I resented that, but I didn't let on. I said, "It was touchier. I'd been quizzing around for about a week in town and at some of the ranches. I was ready for bed one night when I heard a knock on my door. I opened it. Five men were in the hall. They didn't wait to be asked in. They pushed me out of the way and came in and closed the door.

"They all wore masks, they carried guns, and one of them held a coiled rope that he kept slapping against one leg. They said the trouble in Johnson County had been over with for ten years and they didn't want the hard feelings started up again, especially by a snot-nosed reporter from Denver. There was a stage out in the morning for Casper at seven o'clock. If I wasn't on it, they'd be back."

"You don't tell all of that," he said, tapping the sheets of paper.

"No, sir," I said. "I was sent there to see if the local people still held any hard feelings about the Johnson County war. I reported that."

"You did that." He chewed on his cigar for a

time, then he nodded. “Maybe you’re right. It might make things worse for them if it was known you were threatened. Are you sure they weren’t bluffing?”

“I didn’t figure it was smart to hang around and find out,” I said, “especially since I had what I’d come for.”

He nodded again. “You wonder how human beings can go on hating like that after all these years.”

“They feel very strongly about what happened,” I said. “Some people are still living there who had been on opposite sides. They don’t do any more business with each other than they have to.”

“Now about the sheep war on the other side of the Big Horns,” he said. “I gather from what you wrote that it wasn’t so touchy.”

“No sir,” I said. “The sheepmen are in a minority. I doubt that the killers will be found guilty, although most of the people don’t approve of what happened. I think it will depend on how much evidence is brought out in the trial. When I was there, I had a feeling that some of it was being withheld.”

“All right,” he said, dismissing the whole matter with a wave of his hand. “Now then. You’re leaving on the evening train for Trinidad. This may be a tough assignment. Take your hand gun and your Winchester. I don’t know how long this job will be, but I have a hunch you may wind up in a pot of trouble. It's about Gordy Morgan. It happened a couple of months ago, so maybe you'd read about it before you left for Wyoming."

"I remember something about a couple of killings in a little town called Lark," I said. "I don't recall the details."

"Three killings, to be exact. I was interested in it then, but I didn't want to send anyone else down there and I wanted you to go to Wyoming. The Trinidad *Weekly Tribune* has picked it up and keeps asking where young Morgan is. He's only eighteen, so they're comparing him to Billy the Kid and they're after the sheriff's hide for not nailing him.

"Now I'm not sure he really is a killer. Maybe the paper down there keeps the story alive just to sell more copies. Of course the local people are interested, but maybe somebody wants it kept alive. They're calling young Morgan the Trouble Kid. Well, I'm not sure he caused the trouble in the first place."

He stopped and looked at me to see if I was following him. I had worked for him long enough to know that he had a strange, extra sense about people and the trouble they got into. I said, "You think this Morgan boy isn't guilty and you want me to find out?"

"It's worth looking into," he said. "The part I don't savvy is what's happened to him. Why didn't he stay in Lark and fight it out? Now he's disappeared. I'm wondering if he's been murdered. I want you to find him if he's still alive and talk to him. It may be a long chase. If you don't find anything, come on home. If you do, keep on the trail."

He shoved a couple of envelopes across the desk to me. "Here's expense money. If you need more, wire me." He tapped the other envelope with the tip of an ink-stained finger. "Also some clippings from the Trinidad paper." He leaned back and folded his hands across his paunch. "I haven't had a hunch like this for years, and it's been eating on me. I'd go down there myself if I wasn't so damned old. I think the boy is being harassed. If he has been killed, it's plain murder, probably for revenge. I want to know."

I picked up the envelopes and stuffed them into my pockets. "I'll do what I can, but I don't see why I'll be in so much danger that I need to take my guns."

"Maybe you won't, but take them anyway," he answered. "I guess it's part of my hunch. You're going to be doing a lot of riding, so you'll be exposed. Maybe somebody down there doesn't want the real story to come out. Or maybe they're trying to twist it. You can rent a horse in Trinidad. Or buy one if you think that's the thing to do."

"All right," I said. "If it looks like a long trail, that's what I'll do."

"Good luck, Curran," he said. "Keep the stories coming in. I'm going to have to get a lot of copy out of you to make an investment this large look good."

"You'll get it," I said.

I left the office, caught a street-car to my one-room apartment, and exchanged my dirty laundry for all the clean clothes I could scrape together. I caught the night train to Trinidad. I didn't know it at the time, of course, but this assignment brought about a complete change in my way of life. As a result, this narrative turned out to be more my story than the story of Gordy Morgan.

CHAPTER II

I finished reading the clippings from the Trinidad *Weekly Tribune* before the train reached Colorado Springs. I slipped the clippings back into the envelope and dropped it into my coat pocket, then leaned back and thought about what I'd read. I had the same feeling the Big Man had had, that Gordy Morgan was having the deck stacked against him. Not that anything was said directly that made me think that. It was a hunch, too, I guess. I'd been on this type of assignment long enough to get hunches that proved right more times than they were wrong.

Actually none of the clippings gave the full story, or why the law wasn't after Morgan. It seemed pretty evident that the law didn't consider him guilty. Not that he hadn't done the killings. But murder and killing are two different things. It struck me that he possibly, even probably, acted in self defense. Why, then, was the *Tribune* hounding the sheriff for not arresting him?

I could think of several possible answers. One was that the newspaper had a grudge against the sheriff. This was certainly the biggest killing in the county for years, and it was a natural line to take if indeed the *Tribune* was after the sheriff's hide. With elections coming up this fall, it seemed a likely answer, particularly if the newspaper was in the pocket of some other candidate.

I thought of another possibility. I took the envelope out of my pocket and read the first clipping again, one that was dated back in July. It said: "Gordon Morgan shot and killed two cowhands employed by the Rafter P as they were allegedly entering his home near Lark. This happened early Thursday morning last, a few hours after his brother Dave had been wounded during an altercation at a dance in Lark. That same evening young Morgan shot and killed Bud Pettit, the only son of Saul Pettit, owner of the Rafter P."

The article went on to say that Gordon Morgan had disappeared and no doubt Sheriff Carlos Garcia would soon capture the killer and incarcerate him. None of the later articles gave any more details about the actual shootings, but, as time passed, the newspaper became more strident in denouncing the sheriff for failing to do his duty.

Not once was any reason given for Garcia's failure to arrest Morgan. He was simply blamed for not doing it. The last clipping termed Garcia's performance outrageous and said that Morgan was probably in Mexico before this and that it was more than time for a change in the sheriff's office.

I suspected that both of my guesses were true. I could certainly see Saul Pettit's hand behind the newspaper's attitude. It seemed obvious that he would want Morgan arrested, tried, and convicted of his son's killing. If he was a man of some power and prestige, he could very well influence the newspaper's stand. Too, it struck me as interesting that there was an editorial slant to all of the news stories about Morgan.

Finally I gave up thinking about it and dropped off to sleep, my head resting on the red plush of the back of my seat. I was dead tired and I suppose I snored, but there was only a handful of people in the coach, so I didn't worry about bothering them. Most of them were asleep anyway.

I woke up in time to hear the conductor call, "Trinidad. All out for Trinidad." The sun was beginning to show above the eastern horizon when I checked into the Columbian Hotel. I took a room, slept until noon, then shaved, dressed, and had breakfast. I had been in Trinidad before, so when I left the hotel, I had no trouble locating the courthouse.

I found the sheriff, Carlos Garcia, in his office, a stocky man with a bushy black mustache. I introduced myself, gave him my card, and told him I was there to get a story about the Gordon Morgan shootings in Lark.

Garcia was surprised. He motioned me to a chair, offered me a cigar, and said, "I don't savvy why you're here. It happened almost two months ago. It ain't what I'd call news any more."

"I would have been here sooner," I said, "except that I was in Wyoming on another assignment. I guess my boss figured I was the man for the job. Besides, Morgan has never been caught and tried. It seems a little mysterious."

Garcia looked at me for a moment, frowning; then he said, "We don't know where Morgan is, or even if he's alive. It's more than likely he's dead. He disappeared right after he shot young Pettit. I guess that does make it a sort of mystery, all right."

I liked Garcia. He was smart and direct, and I took him for an honest man. Sometimes I miss my judgment on people, but I'm conceited enough to believe I'm right about ninety per cent of the time. I wouldn't be alive if I wasn't.

"It does indeed," I said. "My boss has a nose for mystery and strange events. I guess this one finally got to him. He said he'd have come himself, but he was too old." I paused, then added, "I don't think he would have sent me at first even if he hadn't wanted me to go to Wyoming. It's been going on for weeks. I guess that's why he got interested."

"I suppose he's been reading our splendid little weekly," Garcia said with a good deal of bitterness, "and he wonders why it's been frying my ass ever since it happened."

"That question did occur to him," I said.

"No secret about it," he said. "You may have guessed the answer. The *Tribune* is supporting my opponent, a man named George Norcross, who runs a fair-sized spread about ten miles east of town. Personally I never had got along with the editor. He bucked me when I ran the first time. Also Saul Pettit owns part of the paper and he ain't no friend of mine, either."

"The hell," I said, thinking that the fact Saul Pettit owned part of the *Tribune* might explain several things.

That was plenty of answer to one question, but I had another. I said, "One aspect of this seems strange. Why didn't you bring Morgan in and hold him for trial? It's the only way to clear him if there's any question about his guilt."

"There ain't any question," he said. "It was self defense. If Bud Pettit had been anybody's son but Saul's, the whole thing would have been dropped weeks ago."

"Why are you so sure it's self defense?" I asked.

"As soon as I heard about the shootings," he said, "I rode to Lark and investigated. It ain't often you get four killings in this county all in about twenty four hours, so . . ."

"Four killings?" I interrupted.

Garcia nodded. "Gordy's brother Ed was stabbed at the dance. That's what started the whole fracas. He died later that same night. I have a deputy in Lark I trust. He had looked into the killings before I got there and he was convinced that Gordy wasn't guilty of anything worse than defending his own life and property. We decided it was justifiable homicide. The law don't want Gordy Morgan, Mr. Curran. It's just the damned *Tribune* that's keeping the whole thing alive."

He leaned back and stared at me somberly. I still wasn't satisfied. It seemed to me that the outcry could have been stopped right away if Morgan had been arrested, tried, and acquitted. It didn't take long to arrive at the conclusion that Garcia and his deputy had a reason for not continuing with the investigation. I didn't want to press Garcia just then, so I waited, sensing that he had more to say.

He did, finally, though he must have just sat there staring at me for a full minute as if trying to decide how much more to add to the story. Or maybe he was trying to read my mind. I've been told I have a poker face, so he might have been having trouble figuring out how I was reacting to what he'd said.

"I could tell you more about the situation in Lark," he said, "but if you're going to follow this all the way to the end, and I sure as hell don't know where the end is, you'd better ride out to Lark and see what you can dig up."

"I aim to," I said, "but I still don't know why you never went after Morgan."

"No sense going after a man if you don't want him for nothing," he said. "Like I said, the killings were in self defense."

"You have no idea where he went?"

Garcia shook his head. "By the time I got there, he'd been gone for more than a day and a night. Nobody around Lark even knew what direction he took when he rode out of town. I would have questioned him if he'd stayed, but as it was, I took my deputy's word."

"He makes himself look guilty just by riding off the way he did."

Garcia shook his head. "Not to me he don't. You don't know Saul Pettit. He never figured his kid ever did anything wrong in his life, but hell . . ." He stopped and shook his head again. "Well, you'll find out about that when you get to looking into the situation in Lark."

"What's your deputy's name?"

"Zach Wheeler. He runs the general store in Lark."

I shook hands with Garcia, telling him I'd see him again after I got back from Lark, and left his office. For a time I stood in front of the court-house looking along the brick-paved street, the hot sun pouring down on me. Garcia had seemed straightforward and honest, but the fact remained that after talking to him, I had wound up with more questions than answers. Apparently he had made no effort to find young Morgan, and nothing he had said really explained that.

I finished my cigar, threw the stub into the street, and turned toward the office of the Trinidad *Weekly Tribune.*

CHAPTER III

I didn't really expect to find anything in the *Tribune* that I didn't already know, but I was curious about the kind of man who had made up his mind about Gordy Morgan and had found him guilty. I also had a notion that I might turn up something in the recent issues of the *Tribune* that the Big Man had missed.

The editor was seated in the back of his cluttered shop, a half-smoked cigar in his mouth, feet on the desk. He was a portly man of about fifty, pale-faced from being inside too much, with an air of being too sure of himself to suit me, a judgment I had already made from his writing.

I told him who I was and gave him my card. He stood up, studied the card for a moment, then held out a fat hand. "Jack Knight," he said, and motioned to a chair. "Sit down."

He dropped into his swivel chair and leaned back, his dark little eyes fastened on my face as he waited for me to state my business. He was suspicious, I thought, and when I said, "I'm down here to find out anything I can about Gordy Morgan," the suspicion flowed across his face as plainly as if it had been written there.

"Now what the hell business is it to the *News* what happens down here?" he demanded. "We're a long ways from Denver."

"You know Roscoe Gentry?"

"I know him," he said as if he wished he hadn't.

"He figures the *News* is interested in anything that happens in the Rocky Mountain region," I said. "Or anywhere in the West for that matter. I just came back from Wyoming on an assignment he'd given me."

"We print all the news from this end of the state," he said in a surly tone. "Go back and tell him to read the *Tribune* if he wants to know what's going on down here. I don't send a reporter to Denver to dig into their news. Tell him to keep his nose out of ours."

"As a matter of fact," I said, "he does read the *Tribune*. That's how he heard about Gordy Morgan."

“Then you know he’s wanted for murder?”

I shook my head. “I’ve been talking to the sheriff. He says the law doesn’t want him.”

“Which same proves he’s a lousy lawman and we’ll be getting a new one come November,” Knight said.

“It strikes me you’ve already tried and convicted Morgan,” I said.

“Oh no,” he snapped. “All we’re saying is that Morgan should have been jailed and held for trial. It’s up to the court to decide if he’s guilty of murder, and if Garcia is guilty of malfeasance for not bringing him in.”

I couldn’t argue with that. I said, “Still, it seems to me you’ve been hitting Garcia pretty good. Maybe you’re more interested in getting him out of office than trying Gordy Morgan.”

“We’re interested in both,” Knight said. “It’s no secret that we’re supporting Garcia’s opponent. Now, if that’s all . . .”

“Not quite,” I said. “I’d like to look at all of the issues of the *Tribune* since the Lark killings.”

“Help yourself.” He pointed to a shelf on the wall that was piled high with newspapers. “They’re all there. Don’t get ’em out of order.”

“I’ll be careful,” I said.

I lifted off the top eight papers and sat down on a stool near a window. I read everything that was in those papers relating to the killings and to Lark. There was a column of Lark news in every issue written by a man named Jonathan Aldridge. I was interested in the fact that the Lark column was better written than anything Jack Knight wrote.

Actually very little was said in the Aldridge columns about the killings. He wrote mostly about the high school graduation—I noted that Gordy Morgan, his brother Ed, and Bud Pettit were all members of the graduating class—dances, church meetings, the comings and goings of Lark people, and occasional visitors.

I also noted that Saul Pettit and the Rafter P ranch were mentioned at least once in every column, and a long account was given of Bud Pettit's funeral. On the other hand, the funerals of the two Rafter P ranch hands who had been shot and of Ed Morgan received one paragraph each.

I did catch one item that the Big Man had missed, probably because he didn't think it had any connection with Gordy Morgan. Maybe it didn't, but it struck me as interesting, largely because of the timing.

Two weeks after the killings in Lark a man was shot and killed in the Columbian Hotel. He had not been identified. The murder was unsolved, but it seemed strange that the men in whose room the body was found had disappeared. He had not been identified, either, except that he was young, tall, redheaded, and had about two weeks stubble on his face. He had signed the register as

John Smith and had given Denver as his address.

I sat there a good ten minutes, I guess, thinking about the murder—if it was that. It, too, may have been a matter of self defense. In any case, Knight wasn't hammering on this killing the way he was on the Lark shootings. It was not even mentioned after the one article that told what had happened.

The timing was what intrigued me. This happened two weeks after the killings in Lark and the stubble on the room occupant's face was estimated to be two weeks old. I knew I was reaching for straws. The clerk could have been wrong on his estimate. It probably was a coincidence. Still, I made up my mind to talk to Garcia about it.

Before I left I thanked Knight who grunted a "You're welcome." I started to walk away, then stopped. "Garcia told me that Saul Pettit owns part of this newspaper."

He jumped as if he'd been stung by a bee. "Well, what about it?"

"Is it true?"

"Yes, it's true, if it's any of your business. He owns half and I own the other half. Everybody in Trinidad knows that."

I doubted it but I didn't argue. I went on toward the door and had nearly reached it when Knight yelled, "You be careful what you write about me and Pettit!"

I turned, one hand on the knob. "That a threat?"

"You can call it that."

"Then you just scared the hell out of Roscoe Gentry," I said, and left the shop.

I went back to the sheriff's office, but Garcia had gone. I didn't think it was important enough to go to his home. I could see him in the morning before I left town. I had dinner in the hotel dining room, had a drink in the bar, and walked along Main Street until I found a livery stable where I made arrangements to rent a horse the following day.

It was dark by the time I returned to the room. I unlocked the door and stepped in; I caught a glimpse of someone standing just inside the door and tried to jump back, but I was too slow. The roof fell in on me.

When I came to, I was lying on the floor beside the bed. The door was closed, but there was a faint gleam of light coming in through the window. I had a whopping headache. It was so bad I couldn't think of anything else for awhile. I crawled to the bed and pulled myself up on it and lay down. I'd been hit on the head before, but this was the worst.

I lay there a long time before I felt like stirring. I finally got up, turned on the light, and poured water into the wash basin on the bureau. When I looked into the mirror, I saw that a long streak of blood darkened the right side of my face. I had a sizable lump on the top of my head. I washed, thankful that I'd been wearing my hat when I was struck or I would have been hurt a lot worse.

I thought about the man who had been killed in a room in this same hotel and wondered if there was any connection between that killing and the attack on me, but that seemed pretty far fetched. I thought about going after Garcia, but I didn't feel like it. Anyhow, I didn't see what he could do now. Whoever had hit me was long gone before this, so I decided to go to bed.

It wasn't until I had undressed and turned the covers back that I discovered the note pinned to one of my pillows. It was brief and to the point: "Go on back to Denver. Leave the Morgan killings to the people who are concerned."

I sat on the edge of the bed for a long time staring at the note. It didn't tell me anything. It was scrawled in pencil on a piece of cheap paper that had probably been torn from some child's school tablet. But I was sure of one thing: Jack Knight had to be the man who was responsible for the attack on me. No one else knew why I was here except Garcia and he would have had no reason to scare me off the Morgan case. At least I couldn't think of any reason he'd have. He'd been friendly. Knight hadn't.

I was sure of one other thing, too. My gun was in my valise, but from now on I'd be wearing it. Roscoe Gentry had been right.

CHAPTER IV

My head hurt so much I slept very little until nearly dawn, when it began to taper off into a dull ache. I finally dropped off to sleep and didn't wake up until after eight. I got up, shaved, dressed and had breakfast. By that time I felt pretty well—at least well enough to ride.

I paid for my room. Not knowing how long I'd be gone, I asked the hotel clerk to store my valise. I was wearing my Colt and carrying my Winchester along with a war bag that held a few necessities such as my shaving gear and a couple of clean shirts. The clerk looked me over, making no attempt to hide his curiosity. I guess he thought it was peculiar for a city man to be wearing a six gun and carrying a Winchester.

I thought about giving him my opinion of the lock on my door, but decided I didn't want to tell him about the attack on me, so I kept still. Actually the lock was no better or worse than the lock on a door in any western hotel. Most of them could be opened with an ordinary skeleton key. The trouble was I hadn't expected to be attacked and I still didn't make any sense out of it. I just couldn't see that Jack Knight had anything to gain.

It was mid-morning by the time I got my horse,

tied my war bag behind the saddle, and slid my Winchester into the scabbard. I rode to the courthouse, tied, and went into the sheriff's office. A swarthy-skinned deputy sat at a second desk in a corner of the room. Garcia introduced us and motioned to a chair.

"Headed for Lark?" he asked.

"That's right," I answered.

He motioned toward my Colt. "I guess you're ready for trouble."

"I've had trouble," I said. "That's why I stopped in this morning."

I told him what had happened. He seemed surprised, then shook his head. "I should have told you more than I did yesterday, but I didn't think this would happen. I don't like to pass rumors along. The fact is we don't really know what's going on. We pick up stories and it's hard to know what's true and what's a lie."

He rose and walked to a window where he stood staring out into the yard. Finally he asked, "Who did you tell besides me why you're here?"

"Nobody but Jack Knight," I said.

He wheeled to face me. "You couldn't have told anybody worse," he said. "He's like this with Saul Pettit." He held up two fingers pressed tightly together. "Pettit calls the turn. Knight is nothing more than an echo."

"He seemed hostile," I said, "and he warned me to be careful what I wrote about him and Pettit."

"He's great on warning," Garcia said somberly, "and once in a while it's a good thing to listen." He sat down at his desk and made a steeple out of his fingers. "You've got to know Saul Pettit to understand our situation, and I reckon you won't be around Lark very long until you know quite a bit about him. He's the most powerful man in the county financially and politically. I'm surprised I was elected sheriff in the last election and I'll be more surprised if I win the next election.

"Now this is more or less the way a lot of counties are in the cattle country. We've got mining interests here, too, and he's into them. He owns most of the bank and serves on the board of directors. But he's different from the big men in other counties. He's a madman. Now that's hard to savvy because in most ways he's normal. He's a very sharp business man, but there's a side of him that's loco. He considers himself above the law. I guess he thinks he can make his own laws.

"That's where Gordy Morgan comes in. You see, Pettit had only one son and Gordy shot him. Pettit worshipped the boy who was, from what I've heard, a genuine son of a bitch. The only thing Pettit can see is that Gordy's a murderer and he's going to execute him. I know you've been wondering why we didn't make any effort to bring Gordy in. There are three reasons.

"In the first place we didn't know where he went. He seems to have jumped into a hole and pulled it in after him, but even if we had known where he went, we wouldn't have brought him to town and jailed him. That brings us to the second reason. By the time I got to Lark, Zach Wheeler had investigated the whole business and had made up his mind that all three killings were justifiable homicides. When he told me what he had found out, I agreed.

"If we had brought Gordy in, he would have been dry-gulched on the way to town, or he'd have been broken out of jail and lynched. We couldn't have got any help here in town. Not against Saul Pettit."

He rose and walked to the window again. The deputy was leaning back in his chair and smoking a cigarette, his eyes on Garcia. I began to think that perhaps Jack Knight was right, that it did add up to malfeasance in office—but then, I wasn't in Garcia's place.

He turned around and faced me. "Maybe you're thinking I was looking out for myself, not wanting to fight off the Rafter P crew and get myself and my deputy killed. Well, I reckon I was, but I was also thinking of Gordy Morgan. He wouldn't have had a chance. And that brings me to the third reason. If he had gone to trial, he would have been convicted. That's as certain as the sun is going to come up in the morning."

I don't know what I would have done if I'd been in Garcia's boots. Anyhow, it wasn't my job to judge him. I still didn't know the whole story, but I would before I left Lark. If the three killings were justifiable homicide, then I'd have to agree with what Garcia had done. At least Gordy Morgan was alive, and Garcia was saying as plainly as he could that the kid would be dead if he'd been jailed.

"Do you think it's possible that Morgan came to Trinidad after the killings?" I asked.

He nodded. "It's possible. He'd never been to town and not many around here know what he looks like. I don't know what his thinking might have been, but maybe he just didn't know where to go. He didn't have any friends except the ones in Lark and he couldn't go back to them. Maybe he just came in to get supplies and think things over."

"What about the killing in the hotel six weeks ago?"

"How did you know about that?" he demanded. "It never got the publicity the other killings did."

"I went through the last eight issues of the *Tribune*," I said. "I wondered why more wasn't said about it in the paper. It seems that Knight wanted to say as little as possible about it while he kept hammering on you and the Morgan boy."

"That's right," Garcia said. "Well, we don't know much about that killing. I questioned everybody around the hotel who had seen the man who was renting the room where the body was found. I did learn he had left his horse in Brady's livery stable, but he took him out before daylight and left."

"You think he might have been Morgan?"

"Maybe, but I don't have any notion about why he killed this man. That is, any notion I can prove." He paused, eyeing me speculatively for a moment; then he asked, "You know anything about the De Bussy Detective Agency in Denver?"

"I sure do," I said. "They're a bunch of damned cutthroats, and Hank De Bussy is the worst cut-throat of the lot. He used to be Soapy Smith's right-hand man, then after Soapy left Colorado, he tried to take over the criminal business in Denver, but he couldn't swing it, so he started his detective agency—which I consider a murder-for-hire outfit, though I can't prove it."

"I'm not surprised," Garcia said. "This is the part I should have told you yesterday. The rumor is that Pettit has hired the De Bussy people to find Gordy Morgan. If they do, it's my guess they'll kill him, so the chances are it was one of De Bussy's men who slugged you last night. We've had several strangers around town the last few weeks. We don't know, but we suspect they're some of De Bussy's detectives."

"I still don't savvy why they'd attack me," I said.

"I told you that you had to know Saul Pettit to understand this," he said. "He wants Gordy

Morgan himself. He don't even want us to bring him in. He says he will be the executioner."

I could see several angles to that statement and it took me a little while to think it over. Finally I rose. "I'd better ride if I'm going to get to Lark tonight."

"You can see where this is taking you, can't you?" Garcia asked. "We can't protect you."

"I can see several things," I said, "and none of them look logical."

"They ain't," Garcia said. "That's why I said Pettit is a madman. Madmen are not logical. I advise you to go back to Denver."

"Thanks for the advice," I said, "but I'm looking forward to meeting Saul Pettit."

I left the office with the strong impression that both Garcia and his deputy thought I was a madman or maybe just a plain damn fool for going to Lark. I wasn't either one. When that son of a bitch slugged me, he brought me into the game. I wasn't just a reporter now. I was a participant.

CHAPTER V

The road to Lark led directly east from Trinidad. To the north the arid plain broke away toward the Picketwire that angled northeast to the Arkansas; to the south a low range of mountains lay along the Colorado-New Mexico line, stretching from Fisher Peak which dominated Trinidad to the low rolling hills south of Lark. I passed a number of ranches, small outfits whose owners were undoubtedly barely hanging on, but as I approached Lark, I noted there were no ranches at all.

I reached the town late in the afternoon and found it to be even less of a settlement than I had expected. The business block, if it would be complimented by calling it that, consisted of a saloon, a general store and post office, a livery stable, and a blacksmith shop. On beyond by perhaps fifty yards were a school building on one side of the street and a church on the other.

Turning into the livery stable, I stepped down and told the hostler to give the horse a double bait of oats and that I'd probably be leaving in the morning. Actually I had no definite plans beyond seeing Zach Wheeler, but at the moment I didn't see much use of staying here.

I untied my war bag from behind the saddle and pulled my Winchester out of the scabbard, then I asked, "Any place in town I can get a room?"

"The saloon's the only place," he said. "You can get meals, too. Ain't long on quality, but there's plenty of it."

"Did you know Gordy Morgan?" I asked.

He had started to lead my horse into a stall, then he stopped and stared at me. He said, "Yeah, I knew him."

"What sort of a boy was he?"

"I ain't saying anything," he answered, "except that it is a hell of a situation that drives a boy like Gordy out of town and he can't even get a trial to clear hisself. Now don't ask nothing more 'cause I ain't got nothing more to say."

I turned toward the archway, knowing there was no use pressing the man. He probably couldn't say anything without making a commitment one way or the other, and he didn't want anything he said to get back to Saul Pettit.

I walked directly to the saloon, thinking that I'd better get my room before I went to see Zach Wheeler. The bartender was a man in his sixties, baldheaded and bearded, with a round ball of a belly.

"Yeah, sure," he said when I asked for a room. "There's four of 'em upstairs. Take your pick."

The saloon was typical for an out-of-the-way community like Lark. The bar was composed of two pine planks laid across saw horses, four faded, green-topped tables, several bracket lamps on the walls, and, behind the bar, a fly-specked painting of a fat, naked woman, one hand extended in a beckoning gesture.

I climbed the stairs at the back of the saloon and selected a room in front that looked down on the street. To my surprise the room was clean. I turned back the covers, wondering if I'd do better in the livery stable mow, but the sheets were clean.

The mirror hanging on the wall above the bureau was cracked, but it gave back a clear, sharp reflection. A pitcher on the bureau was filled with water, a wash basin was beside it, and there was a thunder mug under the bed and a slop jar beside the bureau. All the comforts of home, I thought, but I had to admit I had seen worse.

Leaning my Winchester against the wall, I tossed my war bag and hat on the bed, then washed, slapped my hat back on my head, and went downstairs. I said, "I've got an errand to run, but I'll be back for supper."

"Sure, sure," the bartender said. "I'll fix you something. I ain't no real cook, but I've been staying alive on my vittles for sixty year."

I went back into the street, thinking there probably weren't more than ten houses in town, most of them built of logs. A rider was coming in from the south, so there had to be at least one spread somewhere back in the hills. I wondered what the Rafter P hands did when they went on a toot. I couldn't see much in Lark for them, so they probably made up for it when they went into Trinidad.

I crossed the street to the general store. It was typical of stores in towns like Lark, the dry goods on one side, groceries on the other, and a potbellied stove in the back beside a rolltop desk. I caught the same odors I had smelled in similar stores, a strange smell that I never found in any other place except small-town stores. It couldn't be defined, simply because it was a combination of so many smells originating from leather and neatsfoot oil and bolts of cloth to pickles, cheese, and crackers, all caught in a relatively small room that was never thoroughly aired. It was not an offensive smell, just peculiar.

"Anybody here?" I yelled.

A little man wearing a star on his vest rolled out of the back room. That is, he was short-legged and fat, and there was something about his gait that made him appear to roll instead of walk. He was in his middle fifties, I judged, with pink cheeks and a bristly mustache that would have given some men a fierce expression but only made him look comical.

"Yes sir," he said in a chirpy voice, "somebody is here. What can I do for you?"

I gave him my card, thinking that if I'd been looking for a deputy, he was about the last man in town I would have picked. I offered my hand, saying, "Sheriff Garcia said you'd talk to me. I just rode in from Trinidad."

He shook my hand, his grip surprisingly strong, looked at the card as if puzzled, then at me, and back at the card again. He said, "Sure, you can talk to me, but what I say to you depends."

"The sheriff said you handled the Gordy Morgan killings," I said. "That's what I came to talk to you about."

That startled him. He backed away from me, shaking his head. He said, "You're from the *Rocky Mountain News*. I want to know why you're poking your nose into something that ain't one damn bit of your business."

"My boss figured it was our business," I said. "He thinks there's a story here that hasn't been told and I'm supposed to get it."

"Gordy Morgan has been kicked around enough by the *Tribune*," Wheeler said bitterly. "If you think I'm gonna say one word that will let you make it tougher on him than it already is, you're loco."

"Did it ever occur to you that what I dig up and the story I write might make it easier on Morgan?"

"Well no, it didn't," he said. "Not after the way the *Tribune* took after him." He scratched his head, frowning thoughtfully. "You know, that damned *Tribune* never has told what really happened. Maybe Knight don't know, or maybe he don't want to know. Anyhow, he never came out here to talk to me."

"Do you know what really happened?"

"Not exactly," he admitted, "but I reckon I know more'n anybody else except Gordy."

"Here's your chance to get what you know into print," I said.

"I don't have no way of knowing you'll tell it straight," he said.

"That's a chance you'll have to take," I said,

"but I can tell you one thing. I'm not on Saul Pettit's side." I told him what had happened to me in my hotel room in Trinidad, and added, "It doesn't take more than one beating like that to make me think something's wrong with the way things stand. Somebody, and it would have to be Pettit, wants the lid kept on, so it strikes me he's afraid for the truth to get out."

"Exactly," Wheeler agreed. "I tell you what we'll do. You go back over to the saloon and get your supper. I'd take you home with me, but the old lady gets on her high horse when she don't know we're having company. I live right back of the store. You come over in an hour or so and we'll talk."

"I'll be there," I said.

I left the store and crossed the road to the saloon, noting that one horse was tied at the rail. He wasn't there when I left the saloon, so I guessed that the rider I had seen coming in from the south had arrived and was having a drink.

When I went in, I saw the man at the bar, tall and thin and old with a white beard and faded blue eyes that looked me over curiously as I walked toward him. He had an empty glass in front of him and was twirling it with the tips of his fingers. His clothes were patches on patches, so I had a hunch he wanted a drink and was too broke to buy it.

"Whisky," I said to the barkeep, and nodded at the old man. "Join me?"

"You bet," he said eagerly. "Glad to."

"He would," the bartender said sourly as he poured the drinks. "He's been badgering me about a drink ever since he came in. If he paid up for what he owes me, I could show a profit for the year."

"I'll have my supper," I said.

He nodded. "I'll go stir the fire up. It'll be half an hour."

The old man had downed his drink and had shoved his glass at me as if hoping I was going for another one. I said to the bartender, "Before you go, pour my friend another drink."

"Sure," the barman said, "if you're paying."

"You've got no call to be so damned stingy," the old man said in an aggrieved tone. "I've paid for enough drinks right here in this saloon for you to show a profit for the last ten years."

The bartender walked into the back room without adding anything more to the conversation. "Damned skinflint," the old man muttered. "When I had money, he was my best friend. Now I don't, he's got no more time for me."

"You live hereabouts?" I asked.

He jerked a thumb to the south. "Got me a cabin back there in the hills. I used to have me a little spread, but old Saul, he gobbled me up like he's done everybody else. They all pulled out but me; I hang on. I'll die out there someday. I reckon it don't make no difference where a man dies."

"You know Gordy Morgan?" I asked.

I knew from the expression on his wrinkled face as soon as I said it that it had been the wrong thing to say. He'd been stretching his hand out toward the bottle that the bartender had left in front of me. It froze, hand palm down on the bar as he stared at me, a crazy, wild expression coming into his eyes, then without a word he wheeled and ran out of the saloon, got on his horse, and galloped away, heading south the way he had come.

When the bartender came back, he said, "What happened to old Pete? I'm surprised he left. He figgered he had a good thing going with you."

"He took off like he had a firecracker fizzing on his tail," I said. "I just asked him if he knew Gordy Morgan."

It was the bartender's time to stare at me as if he couldn't believe he'd heard right; then he said, "Mister, you're a long ways from home. If you want to get back all in one piece, you'd best not ask about Gordy Morgan. Mr. Pettit, he figgers that's his business and nobody else's. Gordy killed his boy, you know. He's hurting real bad, Mr. Pettit is."

I nodded as if I understood. I guess I did. I was going to have trouble learning anything I didn't already know beyond what Zach Wheeler would tell me. The stableman hadn't wanted to talk. Now with old Pete taking off the way he had and the bartender adding his little piece of advice, I began to wonder if even Wheeler would talk freely.

CHAPTER VI

Zach Wheeler's house was a modest log building, about four rooms, I judged. His business, I thought, must not be the best. He opened the door to my knock and motioned me to a chair. His furniture was as modest as his house. There were two rocking chairs, two straight-backed chairs with woven cane seats, an imitation leather couch, and a claw-footed walnut stand in the middle of the room. The floor was covered by a rag rug.

He got out his pipe and filled it, eyeing me as he tamped the tobacco down, then he struck a match and lit it. He said, "I reckon you want the whole story?"

I nodded. "All that you know."

"Well, we'll have to go back a piece," he said. "You see, Gordy's father, Link Morgan, and Saul Pettit were friends in the beginning. They grew up together in Ohio and went to the same school. They fought through the Civil War in the same company. When they went home after the war was over, they weren't satisfied to go back to the farms they grew up on. Along with four or five others from the same part of Ohio, they came out to Colorado.

"They settled on the Arkansas and later on Link and Saul Pettit came down here. Saul settled north of town a couple of miles. Still has his headquarters ranch there. Link, he was what you might call a free soul. He was never one for working. He was capable enough, but he never wanted much from life except to be allowed to live the way he wanted to. He settled in the hills south of town where he could hunt. He bought a few cows and built a stone house and later on got married.

"Link's wife was a fine woman. Belonged to one of the early families in this part of the country. She didn't want no fine house or anything, either. Just a home and husband and kids. She had two boys and a girl she lost. She up and died a couple of years ago and Link was a lost man after that. They sure did love each other. Oh, Link had his boys and they got along fine, but nothing was the same after his wife died. He raised his boys to be about like he was, only Gordy was the smart one and Link didn't know what to make of him. He had big hopes for Gordy and wanted to send him to college, but hell, he didn't have much money. A few hundred dollars that he hid in his cabin was his life savings. Anyhow, he got bucked off a horse and died six months ago.

"Now Saul was a different breed of cats. He had more money to start on and he was ambitious as hell. He bought a fair-sized herd of cattle and started expanding almost from the first. In those days there were a lot of small spreads in this country, but most of 'em were starving out and Saul began to buy 'em up. Everything he did seemed to make money for him, and the more he made, the tighter and meaner he got, especially to them that owed him money.

"Trouble with Saul was he couldn't stand anybody bucking him. He had to have his own way or he just plowed you under. The only man who wouldn't sell to him was Link Morgan, and the longer that time went on, the madder he got at Link and the stubborner Link got. Saul owned land on all sides of Link's place which was only a section of land, but that section was like a boil on Saul's ass that'd hurt him every time he sat down.

"Well, Link and Saul got to hating each other something fierce. Saul hated Link because Link wouldn't sell, and Link hated Saul because Saul kept pestering him to sell and made life downright miserable for him. Their boys made it worse. Saul hadn't married for quite a while. His wife didn't live long after they were married. Just long enough to have Bud. He was about the same age as Gordy. They fought all the time. Saul figured Bud was about perfect, but everybody else considered him an ornery son of a bitch. I guess he couldn't help being what he was, spoiled rotten from the day he was born.

"Ed was a year older'n Gordy, but he wasn't as smart as Gordy and he wound up in the same grade. They fought together. Did just about everything together. If one of 'em had trouble, the other one had the same trouble. They were both good boys and folks hereabouts liked 'em the same as they hated Bud Pettit. Bud never went anywhere without two or three of his dad's cowhands, so when there was a fight, it was the two Morgan boys against Bud and some of the Rafter P hands. The Morgan boys always came out losers, being outnumbered the way they were.

"Now we've got a girl named Cissy Edwards complicating the story. She's a purty little filly and knows it. Like I said, I ain't sure just what happened, but I'm purty sure the fights was over her. Her pa is the preacher, but which has nothing to do with it I suppose. Most folks consider Cissy a floozy, though it may just be ugly gossip. Anyhow, Bud and Gordy were both chasing Cissy for all they were worth. I've been expecting trouble for quite a while, but it never came until the night of the dance after high school graduation.

"Our school is a small one with just two teachers in high school and two in grade school. Most of the students come from quite a ways off, so they board here in town while they're going to school. Bud and the Morgan boys lived close enough to town so they always rode their horses to school.

"Bud had the best grades in the graduating class, so he gave the valedictory and he done a hell of a good job. Everybody around here went to the graduation and stayed for the dance afterward. Bud and Gordy got into a row over a dance with Cissy. Maybe she egged 'em on. I think it pleased her female vanity to have the boys fighting over her.

"Anyhow, Bud invited Gordy outside. Gordy was never one to turn down a fight, so he and Ed took Bud up on his invitation. As usual Bud had three Rafter P hands with him. As soon as Gordy and Ed came through the door, they were jumped and in the fracas Ed got stabbed. Maybe by Bud, though I don't know that for sure.

"We've had a rule here for a long time that nobody carries a gun in the gym during a dance but me. When I found out what had happened, I ran outside and fired a couple of shots over their heads. That stopped 'em. I told Gordy and Ed to climb on their horses and git for home. You see, I didn't know Ed had been hurt. They done what I told 'em, but when I told Bud and the Rafter P boys to go back into the gym and stay there, Bud got snotty and said he guessed they wouldn't do no such thing. They were going after the Morgans and wind up the trouble for good.

"Well sir, right then I had about all of Bud's orneriness I could swallow. I didn't give a damn what old man Pettit did to me. I don't mind admitting that's what all of us think about when we get a notion to step out of line. Usually we get back into line pronto, but I knew the Morgan boys would wind up dead if I let Bud and his men go, so I fired a shot at Bud's feet. I reckon I didn't miss his big toe by more'n an inch. I told him he'd better do what I told him or the next shot was coming right up his leg and he'd lose something he didn't want to lose! He got into the gym in a hurry, the other Rafter P men right behind him.

"I didn't think much more about it that night, but in the morning I got to wondering if the Rafter P men might have paid the Morgan spread a visit, so I rode out there. I heard shooting when I was still quite a ways off, then I seen smoke rising from the Morgan buildings. I dug in some steel, and pretty soon Bud came riding by me as if the devil was right behind him. When I got to the Morgan house, I found two dead men in the front yard. Both of 'em were Rafter P hands. Gordy was up on the hill above the house digging a grave beside his mother's and pa's graves. When I climbed up to him, I seen that Ed was lying on the ground, stone dead.

"Of course I felt purty bad about it. If I'd known the night before that Ed was hurt bad, we might have saved his life. Looked to me like he'd bled to death on the way out there. Gordy said he didn't know until they'd got almost home that Ed was hurt bad. I asked him about the two dead men in front of the house. He said he saw 'em coming, so he hid among some rocks on the side of the hill above the house and watched 'em. They got down, hollered for him, and finally started to burn the buildings. They fired a shed, then Gordy cut loose on 'em. He got two of 'em before Bud got to his horse and busted the breeze heading for home.

"I stayed and helped him finish Ed's grave. He said he wasn't going to wait for the preacher to come and say a few words. Ed didn't need 'em, but I said the Lord's Prayer anyway, figuring it wouldn't do no hurt. Then I told Gordy that Saul and his bunch would be on his tail in a hurry and he'd better vamoose. He said he would and I came back to town.

"Of course I don't know what Gordy done, but he must have found some place to hide out till dark. The damned fool wanted to see Cissy before he left. He went to her house after dark. Bud was waiting for him and shot at him. I don't know if he was hit or not, but he shot back and he sure didn't miss. He got Bud right in the brisket. He pulled out in a hurry then and I never got a chance to talk to him. I ain't even heard of anybody that's seen him since then."

Wheeler's pipe had been out for a long time. He lit it again, looking at me through the smoke. "That's the story, Mr. Curran. I expect the sheriff told you we decided the killings were justifiable homicide. We talked it over and I told him what I've just told you. We figured the law didn't need to go looking for Gordy. I sure hope he made it into Mexico."

I considered his story for a time, thinking there

were some pretty good-sized holes in it. He'd taken Gordy's word about what had happened at the Morgan place. He had no way of knowing that Bud Pettit had shot first at Gordy when he went to see Cissy. It struck me that Wheeler figured Gordy had done something that should have been done a long time ago in killing Bud Pettit, and he hoped the boy got away scot free.

Finally I said, "I'd like to see the Morgan place. Could you take me out there in the morning?"

He nodded. "Sure. I'll meet you at the livery stable at eight o'clock."

"I'll be there," I said, and rose, then I thought about the old man who had left the saloon in such a hurry. I told Wheeler about him, adding, "I have the notion that nobody in town wants to say anything bad about Saul Pettit, but this Pete was worse than the others. He acted like the whole business was poison."

"It is," Wheeler said. "That was Pete Grimes, by the way. He's been in the country longer'n Saul has. It isn't that nobody can't say anything bad about the Pettits. We all do and Saul expects it, knowing he don't have no friends around here, but he put out the word that nobody talks about Bud's killing. Folks have learned to take him at his word."

I started to ask why Pettit didn't want Bud's killing talked about, but I didn't get the question asked. A woman stood in the doorway, one of the most unattractive women I had ever seen in my entire life. She had white hair that she'd pulled back tight from her forehead and pinned in a knot on the top of her neck. I don't think she had a tooth in her head. She had a surprisingly long nose and a chin that swept out and up so that it gave the strange appearance of trying to meet the tip of her nose.

"You'd be smart to do the same thing, Zach Wheeler," she said in an accusing voice. "You are a fool to run off at the mouth this way to a man you don't know from Adam."

"Yes, Miranda," he said. "I am a fool to run off at the mouth this way. I won't say any more."

I figured it was time to leave. I thanked him and left the house. On the way back to the saloon I mulled over a question that had bothered me most of my life. Why do men like Zach Wheeler put up with women like that wife of his?

CHAPTER VII

When I reached the livery stable the following morning, Zach Wheeler was there waiting for me, his horse saddled. We left town a few minutes later, headed southwest. For the first half mile Wheeler didn't say a word. He stared straight ahead, his mouth drawn down at the corners. Finally he turned his head to stare at me.

"I know what you're thinking," he said. "You're

thinking that I'm a God-damned spineless piece of humanity."

I was startled. My thoughts had been on Gordy Morgan and Saul Pettit. I still hadn't figured out why Pettit didn't want the case talked about. Actually I had forgotten all about Wheeler's tart-tongued wife.

"Now hold on a minute," I said. "You're doing my thinking for me. I'll admit you don't look the way I pictured a deputy would look, but I guess Garcia is satisfied, so why should I think what you said I was thinking?"

"I didn't mean anything about being a sheriff's deputy," he said sharply. "You know damn well what I meant. No man with the backbone of a jellyfish would stand for his wife saying what she done last night. I apologize if that means anything."

"Forget it," I said.

I saw immediately he didn't want to forget it, that he wanted to punish himself, so I added, "The question did occur to me as to why you put up with her."

"That is the question," he said. "I'm damned if I know, except that you get used to being married to someone and you know you're too old to start hunting for another woman. Just habit, I guess." Then, for some reason, he brightened and added, "You wouldn't believe this, Curran, but she does have some good points."

"Then I guess that's why you put up with her," I said. "Now I've got a question. Why doesn't Pettit want this case talked about?"

Wheeler shrugged. "Who knows what goes on in that bastard's mind? It's partly that he just likes to control everything and everybody, and he knows that if he puts out the word for people not to talk, they won't. He likewise gets some fun out of scaring hell out of folks who don't obey every whim he gets." He paused, then added thoughtfully, "But there are a few people in this community who will talk. You'll find 'em if you look for 'em."

"Obviously that includes you," I said.

"I wasn't talking about me," he said. "I'm a little different kettle of fish. Saul don't like me and he don't like Garcia, and he's working like hell to get Garcia out of office come November, but for now I'm wearing the star. Pettit knows that if anything happened to me, Garcia would be over here in a minute."

He laughed softly. "Besides, I'm a sort of Santa Claus. I carry folks at the store when they can't pay. Pettit knows that if he worked me over, it'd be the one thing that would make folks get their tails up."

He pointed to a cluster of buildings that stood at the base of the mesa hill directly ahead of us. "That's the Morgan buildings. Lance was a good man at a lot of things, but he never worked hard at any of ’em. He could sure build a house out of stone. That house is gonna stand there forever. When his wife was alive and he needed money, he’d go anywhere in the county to build a house. Hell, he didn’t need to ranch. He could have made a good living as a stone mason, but he didn’t want to do it.”

We reached the buildings and dismounted. I had a strange, eerie feeling about the place. Maybe it was my imagination, but it seemed to me there was the smell of death here. Certainly there was no visible sign of life. Not even a dog or a cat or a chicken. Somewhere back of the house a door groaned as it swung back and forth in the wind.

In spite of myself a shiver ran down my spine. I said, “I don’t like the feel of things around here.”

“Neither do I,” Wheeler said, “but then I seen two dead men lying there.” He pointed to a spot to my left. “See that pile of ashes? The wind ain’t left much of it, but the day I was here the shed was still burning.”

He nodded toward the hill behind the house. “See that nest of rocks yonder? Gordy was hunkered down behind it when he nailed them Rafter P hands. He was shooting to kill and he done so, but I don’t know why he let Bud get away. Maybe by the time he finished the other two, he was on his horse and moving. It’s downright hard to hit a man on a running horse. Don’t sound like it maybe, but I’ve tried and missed.”

"Ed's buried up there by those rocks?" I asked.

"That's right," Wheeler answered. "It's the family burial place."

I walked around the house, then went into the log barn and looked around. It was little different than a hundred other barns I'd been in on ranches all over the Rocky Mountain country. Dried horse manure and straw were in the stalls and hay was in the mangers. Saddles were on a pole back of the stalls along with two sets of harness. As I stepped back into the sunshine, I saw a wagon that was pulled up beside the north side of the building.

Wheeler had followed me, not saying anything. I asked, "Didn't the Morgans have some stock?"

He nodded. "About a hundred head of white-faces and four or five horses."

"What happened to them?"

"By this time Pettit has slapped the Rafter P brand on 'em," he said sourly. "He knows Gordy won't be back. He's finally got the spread he couldn't buy from Link, but it sure didn't come the way he wanted it."

We walked back to the horses. Wheeler was right, of course. Pettit's son's life was too big a price to pay for any ten-cow spread just to satisfy a greedy whim. Gordy probably wouldn't come back, knowing he wouldn't live through the night once that Pettit knew he was back, but it seemed a shame that he had lost his family home through what seemed to be no fault of his.

It was time I started talking to myself, I thought. A good reporter doesn't get emotionally involved with his story, but I was, maybe because I had known stockmen who were like Pettit. I hated them for their arrogance and greed. Not that they were any different from political bosses or businessmen who were motivated the same way Pettit was. Any human being who is controlled solely by greed probably is arrogant and bears the same stamp Pettit does. It was just a little easier to see how the pattern works in the cattle country.

"What does Gordy look like?" I asked.

Wheeler scratched his cheek thoughtfully. "Well, he's a fine looking boy and the most growed up eighteen-year-old you ever seen. He grew a beard last year and you'd have thought he was ten years older'n he was. Red, it was, though his hair is a light brown. Blue eyes. Got a limp from having his right leg broke when he was a little shaver. Didn't heal quite right, but it never kept him from playing baseball."

"Big?"

"He's tall," Wheeler said. "Six feet or better, but he ain't big, I mean, he's slim."

"What kind of horse does he ride?"

"A bay gelding with a star on his forehead and four white stockings. Lance raised fine horses and Gordy's bay was one of the best."

I turned to the house and opened the front door

and went in. The furniture was still there, probably just like it was when Gordy left. Nothing fancy. A couch that had seen better days, too lumpy to be comfortable, with a couple of springs about to pop through the cloth covering. A rocking chair. A stand in the middle of the room that held a dozen scars and dents. A bookcase that was filled. I glanced at them, noting that most were classics, some history, but mostly fiction and poetry.

"Gordy was the reader," Wheeler said from the doorway. "His mother bought most of the books for him. I don't think Lance knew a book from a hole in the ground."

I walked into the kitchen and on back into the pantry. The shelves were well stocked with groceries. I stepped into both bedrooms and then returned to the living room, thinking I could feel the kind of life the Morgans had had. A good home, a happy home, and it was a terrible tragedy that none of them would ever live here again. I knew one thing for sure. Gordy Morgan was not the Billy the Kid that the *Tribune* had made him out to be.

Suddenly I realized I was on Gordy's side all the way. *Damn it, Curran,* I told myself. *Come down to earth. Gordy Morgan's nothing to you. You've got a story to write.*

But I knew it wasn't going to do any good. If I had any sense, I'd go back to Trinidad, write the story from what I knew, and catch the next train to Denver. But I wasn't going to do any such thing. I had to see and talk to Gordy.

"I'm going to find Gordy," I said. "Where do I start looking?"

We were walking back to the horses when I said that. Wheeler stopped and simply stared at me as if he considered me a raving maniac. All he could say was, "Why?"

"I can't write his story without hearing what he's got to say," I answered.

He shook his head. "You're loco, Curran," he said. "Completely loco. By this time he's in Mexico."

"I don't believe that," I said. "I'm beginning to get a picture of him and I don't think he's going to run that far. He's aiming to come back someday. I don't figure he ever will, but he thinks he will and he doesn't want to get so far away he can't get back."

Wheeler threw up his hands. "You've never seen the boy. You don't know him. What makes you think you can tell me, a man who's known him all of his life, what he's thinking and what he'll do?"

I grinned. I couldn't help it. If I'd been in Wheeler's shoes looking at a reporter from Denver who had just said what I'd said, I would have thought he was as crazy as Wheeler thought I was.

"It *is* a little presumptuous, isn't it?" I said. "I

guess it's just a feeling I've got from what I've heard about him and being here and seeing where he's lived all of his life."

I took my hat off and wiped my forehead. It had turned hot and sweat was running down my face. Another idea was beginning to shape up in my mind, a really crazy one this time—a sort of premonition as if I were looking down a corridor of time and I could see the future.

I said, "I think I can save his life."

"Oh, hell," Wheeler said in complete disgust. "I talked to you last night and I brought you out here thinking you were a reasonably sane man, but you ain't. You ain't reasonable *or* sane."

"Where would I start looking for him?" I asked.

He said, "If Pettit hears about you, which he will if you stick around in this country, he'll kill you. You trying to commit suicide?"

"Maybe I am," I said.

"There's another reason Pettit didn't want this talked about. He's staked Gordy out for himself. He wants to kill the boy. He don't want nobody else talking about it or interfering or doing nothing. It's his game and nobody else's."

"Where will I start looking?" I asked again.

He shook his head and turned away, then he stopped and looked back at me. "No reason why I should keep you alive if you're hankering to die. Chances are he rode up onto the mesa and stayed a while with some of the old codgers that live up there, fellers like Pete Grimes. I don't figure they'll talk to you, but you can try."

"Thanks," I said. "Let's get back to town."

Wheeler didn't open his mouth until we were almost back to Lark. Then he said, "If you're hellbound to go on with this regardless of what Pettit will do to you, you oughtta talk to the schoolmaster, Jonathan Aldridge. I guess he knew Gordy better'n anybody else in town. They spent a lot of time together hunting and playing chess and just gabbing. Aldridge lives beside the schoolhouse."

He paused, scowling as if uncertain about whether he should say anything else or not, then he added slowly, "You might try Cissy Edwards. She feels mighty bad about this whole thing, so I don't know if she'll even talk to you, but she's the only one who knows what happened the night Gordy shot Bud Pettit."

"Thanks," I said. "I'll try both of them. You know, I don't think you believe I'm as crazy as you claim or you wouldn't be trying to help me."

"Oh, you're crazy, all right," he said. "Any man is crazy who goes out of his way to get hisself killed or at best have hell beaten out of him. You'll get one or the other." Then he looked straight at me and added, "But I hope you live to write Gordy's story. I reckon you're the only chance we've got to make that God-damned Jack Knight eat his words."

CHAPTER VIII

I found Jonathan Aldridge working in his garden behind his house, which was directly west of the schoolhouse. I expected to find a pedantic looking man, slender and frail with spectacles that slid down on his nose. I couldn't have been more wrong. He was a big man, not fat, just plain big and muscular, a face tanned to a sort of golden bronze, and no spectacles.

He stopped working and leaned on his hoe handle as I approached him. I said, "I'm looking for Jonathan Aldridge."

"You found him," he said. "What can I do for you?"

"You don't look the way I thought you would," I said. "I've been reading your column in the Trinidad *Tribune.* You write very well, Mr. Aldridge."

"Thank you," he said, and then added as if offended, "What did you expect me to look like?"

I knew I had opened my mouth when I should have kept it shut, but I passed it off by saying, "Maybe like a poet, though I guess no two poets look alike."

"Or maybe like a schoolteacher," he said. "You know I am a teacher?"

"Yes, but it was your writing that impressed

me," I said, "maybe because it was so much better than Jack Knight's."

"Saying that my writing is better than Jack Knight's is no great compliment," he said. "What you're really saying is that you expected me to be a scrawny, prissy-looking man more female than male. Well sir, I am a teacher and a hell of a good one, and I get damned mad at the attitude some people like you have toward schoolteachers. Just because teaching has largely been a woman's occupation all these years . . ." He stopped and burst out laughing. "Here I go, getting on my soap box. Just who the hell are you? I've never seen you in Lark before."

"I rode in from Trinidad last night." I gave him my card. "I'm sorry that I got off on the wrong foot with you. I came to ask a favor and I hope you're not put out so much you'll turn me down."

"Probably not. It's just that it's a sore point with me the way some people equate a man teacher with a kind of third sex. Or a sexless person like preachers." He nodded at the church across the street. "You'll know what I mean when you meet Horace Edwards, if you do. Not that all preachers are that way, and I suppose some teachers are. Anyhow, I *am* a teacher and, by God, I'm not ashamed of it. I may starve to death on what they pay me, and my wife has to teach too so we'll have enough to pay Zach Wheeler what we owe him, but I'm not ashamed."

It struck me that he protested too much, but I didn't want to compound my difficulty with him, so I didn't say anything more. I watched him as he looked at my card, then at me, and back at the card.

"Mmmm," he said. "*Rocky Mountain News*. Well, I'm sorry. I'll have to turn you down. Sure I write well, better than most of you boys on the *News* staff, but I'll have to turn down the offer you are about to make. I like it here, Mr. Curran, and my wife likes it." He shook his head. "No, I'll just have to turn you down."

By this time I was absolutely puzzled by the man. I had never met a stranger character in my life than Jonathan Aldridge, and I didn't know how to take him. He was staring directly at me without a trace of humor on his face, but I couldn't believe he was serious.

"I'm not here to offer you a job," I said. "I want to talk to you about Gordy Morgan. The *News* sent me down here to get the true story about him."

"I see." He stuck my card into his shirt pocket. "How do you like my garden, Mr. Curran? I wish I had running water to irrigate with, but all the water I have is what I pump and that gets to be a chore."

I began to wonder if he was crazy—or was he trying to evade talking about Gordy Morgan? I had to admit it was a good garden, with straight rows of lettuce, radishes, carrots, turnips, and cabbage. Farther back were potatoes and tomatoes, and the far end of his garden plot was covered with a tangle of melon and cucumber vines. There wasn't a weed in sight.

"It's the best garden I've seen this year," I said. "You must spend a lot of time working in it."

"I do," he said. "I like to see things grow. I like to eat what I raise, and I like to sell some of it to Zach Wheeler because it helps a little when it comes to paying the bill. I like to see kids grow up, too, and become men and women. They're like the vegetables I raise in the garden except I don't eat them. I helped raise Gordy Morgan. I helped make him the fine young man he is, and by God, I don't know of a greater tragedy than his having to run off the way he did to keep that devil of a Saul Pettit from killing him."

He threw his hoe down with unnecessary violence. "Let's get out of this heat and go into the house. Sure, I'll talk about Gordy Morgan, but if you don't write what I say the way I say it, I'll hunt you down and tear you limb from limb."

I fell into step with him and we walked to the front door of his house. I am not a small man, but I felt small enough, walking beside Aldridge. I figured he probably could really tear me limb from limb if he set his mind to it.

He opened the front door and motioned for me to go into the house. "Sit down," he said, and called, "Zelda!"

A very pretty woman came out of the kitchen, blonde and slender, but not too slender. She was younger than Aldridge by maybe fifteen years—perhaps thirty-five. She smiled at me and offered her hand as Aldridge said, "This is my wife Zelda. Zelda, I want you to meet Curt Curran from the *Rocky Mountain News*. I thought he wanted to offer me a job, but alas, he's here to do a story on Gordy Morgan."

Mrs. Aldridge's grip was firm; her eyes met mine as her smile faded. "Anything that Jonathan tells you about Gordy is the same as I would tell you, Mr. Curran. We have known the boy for ten years. We knew him in grade school. I taught English and history to him in high school. Jonathan taught him math and science. We know him as well as anyone, but it's going to be hard for you to believe he is as splendid a boy as he is and as Jonathan will tell you."

I was beginning to wonder if Gordy Morgan was real, or an angel disguised as a boy! I said, "I will appreciate anything that you or your husband can tell me."

"You have probably read what the Trinidad *Tribune* has written about him," she said. "All lies. Jack Knight is Saul Pettit's man. It may be true that Gordy shot the three men he is alleged to have shot, but if he did, he *had* to do it." She turned away, adding, "I leave you in good hands, Mr. Curran."

"I expect Mr. Curran is thirsty on a day as hot as this," Aldridge said. "Bring him a glass of buttermilk, Zelda."

"Right away," she said.

"Don't bother," I said as quickly as I could. "I'm not thirsty."

As a matter of fact I was thirsty, but the thought of drinking buttermilk was worse than any thirst I could have suffered. I sat down in a rocking chair as Aldridge lowered himself to a leather-covered couch that groaned under his weight.

"I could talk a long time about Gordy," Aldridge said, "but I suppose what you're interested in is his character and talents, since that is what has been so distorted by the *Tribune*. He was a fine student, the best one we've had since we started teaching here. He was also a good athlete. He had a slight limp as you may have heard, but he was a good enough pitcher to have made any college squad in the State if he went on to college. Now he won't, I'm afraid.

"I taught him to play chess and he soon got so he could beat me. I went hunting every fall with him and his brother Ed, and he got his buck whether Ed or I did or not. He and Ed were the closest of brothers, with none of the rivalry and hostility that brothers often have.

"He loved to write and he wrote well. He kept a diary, but it was more than a diary. I read part of it last winter. If you ever find him, you will probably discover that he kept an account of everything that happened to him concerning the shooting. You can believe it, Mr. Curran. Gordy is not a braggart, and he was never one to defend himself if he did anything that was wrong."

"I'm beginning to wonder if Gordy Morgan has any flaws," I said. "Did he ever do anything wrong?"

"He has flaws, all right," Aldridge said, "if you want to call them flaws. For one thing he would have seduced Cissy Edwards if he could. She was the source of most of the trouble between him and Bud Pettit although there had been a hot rivalry between the two boys all the way back to their grade school days, but no doubt you have heard that part of the story."

I nodded. "I've wondered about Cissy. I've been told she is a flirt."

He smiled. "Yes indeed. Her glance was a come-on. She would give it to Gordy, then to Bud, and then to Gordy again, and neither boy knew which one was her favorite. However, I do not think she is a loose girl."

"Can you tell me exactly what happened the night of the fight at the dance?" I asked.

He shook his head. "No, I cannot. We'd had graduation, then a potluck supper, and we'd started the dance. Zelda was functioning at the punch bowl. I was standing a little behind Zelda talking to the county school superintendent who had come out from Trinidad to attend the graduation. In fact, he gave the commencement address.

"I remember the orchestra was playing a waltz. I heard Bud yell above the music that it was his dance with Cissy. Gordy yelled back that it was his. I didn't hear what was said next, but then both headed outside. Ed was standing by the door. He followed Gordy."

Aldridge paused, leaning back and staring at the ceiling. I waited, not sure what had stopped him, then I thought I knew. He didn't want to place any blame on Gordy, but I had a hunch the boy wasn't as blameless as I had been led to believe.

"I guess you might say that Gordy had another flaw," Aldridge said after several seconds of silence. "He was too quick to pick up a fight, though I never knew him to start one. You see, Bud was a son of a bitch anyway you looked at him. We had more trouble with him in school than all the other boys put together, but I am afraid if I'm going to be real honest that Gordy could have sidestepped some of the fights they had if he had wanted to. He just never wanted to.

"Zach Wheeler stopped the fight that night, and I didn't know until later that Ed had been stabbed and had died. It was Ed's death, I think, more than anything else, that hurt Gordy. Whether he shot at Bud first the following night when Bud was killed is something I can't say, but I suspect that he stayed around here to kill Bud because of Ed's death."

I thought about what he had said for a moment. Aldridge said plainly enough that Gordy wanted to kill Bud Pettit before he left the country, but then, Aldridge didn't really know.

"Zach Wheeler says Gordy has gone to Mexico," I said. "What do you think?"

"No, he hasn't done that," Aldridge said in a tone of conviction. "That would be running, and he was never one to run. Retreat yes. He knew that if he stayed, Pettit would kill him, so he had to get away and hide for a time; but he intends to come back. I'd stake my last nickel on that." He spread his hands. "Don't ask me where he is. I have no idea."

I was gratified to hear Aldridge say exactly what I had figured out about the boy. Probably Wheeler knew it, too, but wanted me to think that Gordy had left the country. Of course Gordy would be safer if people, particularly Pettit, believed he had gone to Mexico.

"Zach Wheeler tells me that Pettit has put out the word for folks not to talk about the case," I said. "Why are you willing to talk?"

"Because I'm not afraid of Saul Pettit," he said quickly. "Most people around here are. You see, I've stood up to that bastard for the ten years I've been here. Bud was in school all that time and I have been principal for the same length of time.

I guess I had Bud in my office at least once a week. I talked to him, I threatened him, and I whipped him many times. Nothing helped, partly because Pettit would show up the next day and try to scare me. Bud kept on being ornery because his dad approved of everything he did."

Aldridge laughed softly. "Saul Pettit didn't scare me then, and he doesn't scare me now."

"Do you have a picture of Gordy?" I asked. "An extra one I can have if possible."

He nodded. "I'll get you one. We had pictures taken of each member of the graduating class and I kept several of each."

He rose, went into another room, and returned a moment later with the picture, which he handed to me, a plain three by five without any frame. I looked at it a moment, thinking he was indeed a good-looking boy. But he looked older than eighteen.

I thanked Aldridge, shook hands with him, and left the house. I could accept everything he had said because it matched what Wheeler had told me, but I still didn't really know what to make of Gordy Morgan.

CHAPTER IX

I crossed the street to the Edwards house and knocked on the door. No one answered, so I knocked again. This time the door was opened by a girl.

"I'm looking for Miss Cissy Edwards," I said.

"I'm Cissy," she said.

She was, as Zach Edwards had said, a "pretty little thing." She wore her blond hair in two braids down her back. She had the breasts and the hips of a woman, and the face of a child. I did not find anything provocative about her at the moment, but she looked as if she had been crying. Under other circumstances and with boys such as Gordy and Bud Pettit, I sensed that she could be a very seductive girl.

I handed her my card, saying, "I'm here to write Gordy Morgan's story. Not the story the Trinidad *Tribune* has been running, but the true story."

"I don't want to talk about it," she said, and started to shut the door.

I blocked it with my foot. "Listen, Miss Edwards . . ."

"Cissy," she said.

"All right, Cissy," I said. "Listen to me before you shut the door. I know almost everything that happened and I don't think Gordy is the trouble kid the *Tribune* is making him out to be, but there are a few details you could fill in for me. You owe that to Gordy, don't you?"

She hesitated, then said again, "I don't want to talk about it."

"Who is it?" a man called from somewhere in the back of the house.

"Some reporter from the *Rocky Mountain News*," she answered.

"What does he want?"

Again she hesitated. We stood that way for several seconds, my foot in the door, Cissy biting her lower lip, her hand on the knob. Finally she said, "He wants to talk about Gordy."

"Let him in," the man said. "You know Gordy better than anyone else."

She stepped back and opened the door. "I don't want to talk about it, pa."

"Of course you do," he said, coming toward me, his hand outstretched. "I'm the Reverend Horace Edwards."

He had a firm grip and I like the way he met my gaze. There was no subterfuge about him, no artificiality. He was a very tall man with a long neck and a narrow face. I could see why Jonathan Aldridge reacted to him the way he did, but I respect a man who is sincere. I sensed that Edwards was sincere, perhaps too sincere because he had the burning eyes of a zealot, and suddenly I felt a great sympathy for Cissy.

"Sit down," Edwards said, motioning to a straight-backed chair. "I didn't catch your name, Mr. . . ."

"Curran," I said. "Curt Curran," and gave him my card.

Cissy began sidling toward the kitchen door. Edwards motioned for her to stop. "Now you just sit down right there, young lady, and answer any questions Mr. Curran wants to ask." He turned to me. "Cissy went with Gordy, you know. She also went with Bud Pettit. She refuses to admit it, but she was the cause of the whole trouble. She's going to have to admit it someday when she receives the Holy Ghost."

"Pa," Cissy cried. "You don't have to talk that way."

"We can't avoid it," he said. "It's part of the problem."

She dropped into a chair and began to cry. I said, "I don't want to cause her any discomfort, Mr. Edwards. I just have a few questions I wanted her to answer."

"Of course, Mr. Curran," Edwards said. "You don't realize this, of course, but it's for her own good. She must confess before she can be redeemed." He sat down between Cissy and the kitchen door. "Go ahead and ask your questions. She's been crying ever since it happened and she'll go on crying until she's been saved and is forgiven, then she'll know a greater happiness and peace than she has ever known before in her life."

She sat motionless, her head bowed, and I began to hate the Reverend Horace Edwards. I said, "Cissy, can you tell me what happened the night Bud Pettit was killed?"

"Of course she can," Edwards said. "She was there. Go ahead, Cissy. Tell him. Tell him how he knocked on your window after you were in bed and you were in your nightgown when you talked to him."

I started to get up, thinking that anything I learned from Cissy would not be worth the agony it was costing her, but she began to talk and I sat back.

"I didn't know what happened that day at the Morgan ranch." She kept her head bowed so I couldn't see her face, but she spoke loudly enough so I heard everything she said. "Not until that evening. I didn't even know that Ed had been stabbed the night before and had died. I didn't intend to make any trouble. I guess I was just flirting the way people accuse me of doing."

"Amen," Edwards said.

"There had been fights between Gordy and Bud before," she went on, "but nothing serious had happened. They hated each other, you know. It went back a long ways. I don't know what it was all about. I just know that I didn't cause the trouble in spite of what pa says. Anyhow, I guess I was pretty upset because I didn't hear from

Gordy all day. I love him and I want to marry him. We would have been married if he had stayed. He wanted to marry me before school was out, but I wasn't ready. Pa didn't want me to leave. Besides, I didn't think I was old enough to be a good wife."

"You aren't," Edwards said testily. "She could have had Bud, too, Mr. Curran."

She looked up, her eyes sparking with anger. "I didn't want Bud! Anyhow, I wasn't going out there and keep house for the whole Rafter P outfit and old man Pettit."

"He's a rich man," Edwards said, "but that's all water over the dam. Bud Pettit is dead."

She bowed her head again. "Bud came to see me about six o'clock that evening. He wanted to know if I'd seen Gordy and I said no. I don't think he believed me. Then he told me about the fight out there at the Morgan place, only he didn't tell it the way Gordy did. He said they just rode up to the Morgan house and Gordy started shooting and he killed two Rafter P hands and Bud said he barely got away."

She stopped and took a long breath. Edwards said, "Go on."

"Bud said he was looking for Gordy and was going to kill him when he found him because Gordy had killed the Rafter P cowboys. He said I was going to marry him, not Gordy, and to tell Gordy that when I saw him. I didn't think I'd ever see Gordy again because I knew he had to leave the country or the Pettit bunch would kill him.

"I went to bed and finally dropped off to sleep. I guess it was about midnight that I woke up and heard someone tapping on my window. I got out of bed and opened it. Gordy was standing there looking up at me. I was scared for him because I was pretty sure that Bud was watching the house. I crawled out through the window and . . ."

"In her nightgown," Edwards interrupted as if he considered her act a mortal sin.

I felt like punching him. I held up a hand for him to keep still and I would have told him to shut up if Cissy hadn't gone on.

"I guess Gordy hugged me and kissed me. I don't remember, but I know I held on to him because I didn't want him to leave me. He told me how Bud and his men started to burn him out, and he shot the two cowboys. He said he didn't even try to shoot Bud when he got on his horse and ran away. He said all he wanted to do was to save his home, then he went ahead and buried Ed. Zach Wheeler came out and they talked about it and he knew he had to leave the country, but he said he wasn't leaving until he saw me.

"I told him I'd get dressed and go with him, but he said that wouldn't do, that he had to run fast and hide and I'd just slow him up. I told him that Bud was looking for him to kill him. Bud must have been listening. He wasn't far away when he yelled for me to move away from Gordy because he was going to kill him right there."

She stopped and began to cry again. Edwards said, "I guess that's about all there is to it, Mr. Curran. Cissy is a willful and stubborn girl, but sooner or later she will confess that she caused the trouble. You can see that . . ."

"Mr. Edwards," I said, so exasperated I had difficulty keeping from slugging him. "I'm sure she was not the cause of the trouble. I've talked to both Zach Wheeler and Jonathan Aldridge, and they both have said that the trouble went back a long ways, just as Cissy said." I rose and looked down at Cissy. "Do you know who shot first?"

"No." She glanced up, tears still dropping from her eyes. She wiped them away with a sodden handkerchief. "All I know is that Gordy gave me a shove, a hard shove because I slammed into the wall and it hurt. I fell to my knees and I heard the shots, then Gordy said the whole town would be there in a few minutes and the Rafter P bunch would be on his tail. He stooped down an helped me up, and kissed me. Before I could say anything he was gone. Pa came out of the house and Mr. Aldridge came across the street. Bud was dead then."

"Did Gordy give you any idea where he planned to go?" I asked.

"No," she answered. "All he wanted was to get away from the Pettit bunch."

"Thank you, Cissy," I said, and left the house.

Edwards followed me outside. He said, "I don't know why you defended the girl, Mr. Curran. Perhaps the trouble did go back a long ways, but she was the trigger that set it off."

I couldn't argue with that, but I stood looking at him and wondering what kind of man he was who wanted to keep on punishing his daughter by telling her she was to blame for the killing of three men.

I said, "Mr. Edwards, if I had a daughter like Cissy who is suffering the agonies of hell that she is, I would try to comfort her instead of torturing her the way you're doing."

His face turned red. He said, "I was just thinking of her immortal soul. She must seek forgiveness."

I turned around and walked away. If I had stood there one more second, I would have hit him.

CHAPTER X

As I walked back to the saloon, I remembered Zach Wheeler saying that Gordy probably couldn't hit Bud when he was running away from the Morgan ranch, that a man on a fast horse was hard to hit. I had wondered about it then because apparently Gordy was an excellent shot. Now I had the answer from Cissy. Gordy hadn't tried to kill Bud. He had only wanted to save his buildings, and once that Bud was on his horse and running, there was no more danger of fire. That was a point for Gordy, I thought.

Actually almost everything I had heard about Gordy since I had come to Lark was in his favor. I still didn't know who had fired the first shot the night Bud was killed, but it was a moot point. Gordy would have been justified in firing first since he knew Bud was gunning for him.

I stopped at the bar and asked for a drink, thinking I would go on up to my room and start writing Gordy's story. So far I hadn't mailed anything to the Great Man, and I was overdue. I had all I needed except an actual interview with Gordy, and I didn't see how I could get that. I wasn't even sure, in view of what I had, that the Great Man would want me to stay on Gordy's trail.

The truth was I just couldn't see that Gordy could say anything that would make his case look any better than it did now. I could certainly say that the law was justified in not holding Gordy, that the charges the *Tribune* had been making were not justified.

I didn't get to my room. Not then anyway. I finished my drink, aware that a couple of cowboys were standing at the other end of the bar. I had glanced at them only casually, but now as I turned from the bar to leave, I saw they were moving toward me.

“You Curran?” one of them asked.

“I’m Curran.” I took a card from my pocket and handed it to the man who had spoken. “From the *Rocky Mountain News*.”

The man looked at the card, then he looked at me, and I was scared. I never duck a fight when the odds are even, but I duck every fight I can when the odds are two to one. Besides, these men were big. They looked mean, too. I’ve been around cowboys all my life, and although I can’t make a generality that would be universally accepted, I can say that the average cowboy is normally a very decent human being. These two, now that I had a close look at them, struck me as being a couple of plug-uglies from Larimer Street in Denver.

“We’ll go get your horse,” the man said. “You’re taking a ride with us.”

“I’m sorry, but I’ll have to turn you down,” I said. “I’ve got a story to write . . .”

“There’s two ways to play this,” the man interrupted. “You can get stubborn. In that case we’ll beat hell out of you and then put you on your horse and take you to the Rafter P. Or you can come along without making no trouble for us. Either way, you’re going to have a little talk with Mr. Pettit.”

I didn’t have any trouble making up my mind. As a matter of fact I had considered riding out to the Rafter P and seeing if I could have an interview with Saul Pettit. Now the opportunity was being dropped into my lap, so there was no point in fighting it. I was relieved, and for a minute I wasn't scared.

"All right," I said, and turned toward the bat-wings.

One man walked to the livery stable with me; the other one dropped behind and picked up the two horses that had been tied at the hitch rail in front of the saloon. The man didn't say anything as we walked and neither did I. He was hostile. That was plain enough, and I didn't know why. If he had been sent on what was merely an errand to invite me out to the Rafter P, he had no reason to be hostile. Indifferent, maybe, but not hostile. I should have known, I guess, that this was more than an errand from the way he laid it out to me back there in the saloon.

We walked through the archway, the second man remaining in the street holding the reins of the other horse. "Saddle this yahoo's horse," the first man called to the liveryman.

We stood there in the runway, neither of us speaking, and I got scared again. I began to see I had been stupid not to catch on right away. I suspected we weren't going to see Pettit. I had a feeling they were taking me out of town to beat me up or kill me.

I thought of going for my gun. They had made no effort to take it from me. That was a clue, too.

They wanted me to make a try for my revolver and that would give them an excuse to kill me. I wasn't an expert. If these men were Pettit's bully boys, which I was sure they were, I would expect them to be experts. I wouldn't have a chance, so I decided to play my cards one at a time. If it came to a showdown, I would go for my gun. Now I'd wait and see how it went.

When the liveryman brought my horse to me, I mounted and rode into the street. The man who had been with me followed, mounted his horse, and we took off across the prairie in a northerly direction. They still didn't say anything and they didn't make any threatening moves. This was just a job to them. I wondered how many men they had killed for Saul Pettit.

My worst fears were not realized then. At least this part of the trip turned out better than I had expected. I had been scared more than once while running down the stories the Great Man had sent me to get and I had been threatened more times than I can count. My stay in Johnson County was a case in point, but none had been like this, maybe because I had never run into a man quite like Saul Pettit who recognized no law but his own desires and whims.

It seemed obvious that the basic trouble between the Morgans and Pettits had been due to the fact that the Morgans had defied Saul Pettit, the one thing he could not abide. No one had hinted that

Pettit had murdered Lance Morgan, but the possibility occurred to me before I reached the Rafter P. The thought brought me no comfort. I had been warned once to stay out of the whole affair. Now I began to wonder if Pettit would take time to warn me a second time.

The Rafter P buildings lay before me like an ugly wart on the face of the prairie. The house was a long log structure that looked as if it had started as a one-room cabin and had been added to as need had arisen. Behind it was an assortment of log buildings, one a barn and another shed that held their machinery, and a variety of smaller ones. To the left of the barn was a maze of corrals. There wasn't a tree or a garden or a flower in sight, nothing except the sagebrush and grass that were natural products of the land—and dust.

The crew was gathered around one of the corrals in which a cowhand was trying to ride a bucking horse. The men were yelling encouragement to the rider or the horse. It seemed that they were about equally divided.

The two men who were with me pulled up in front of the house and dismounted. One of them said, "Get down, bucko."

A man who had been at the corral saw us and strode toward us. I stepped down as the two men led their horses toward a boy who was coming to get them, then they turned and came back to stand behind me.

The man who had left the corral stopped about two paces from me and stood staring at me, his gaze moving from my hat down my body to my boots and back up again. He was, I felt sure, Saul Pettit.

He was a tall, lanky man about sixty, with a tanned face that was chiseled by so many deep lines that he looked like the face of time. He was slightly stooped, his arms that seemed inordinately long swung at his sides. His nose was very long, his chin narrow and sharp.

He wore a gun which was what I expected, but there was something else about him that didn't seem to fit a tyrannical and domineering man who rodded the eastern end of the county the way he did—the melancholy, dispirited air of a badly beaten man.

"I understand I was brought out here to have a talk with Saul Pettit," I said.

"I'm Saul Pettit," he said.

"I'm Curt Curran," I said, extending my hand. "From the *Rocky Mountain News*."

He ignored my hand. "I know who you are and I know you've been asking questions, but I don't know why in hell you're here stirring up a lot of dust."

I dropped my hand, my temper ruffled. "I'm here because my boss sent me here. He had been reading about Gordy Morgan in the Trinidad *Tribune* and he had a hunch that young Morgan was not as guilty as the newspaper made him out to be."

"So he sent you down here to prove that Morgan was innocent?" Pettit asked, his lips tightening until his mouth looked like a scar across his face. "Is that it?"

"That's it," I said.

Pettit stood motionless, staring at me. The racket at the corral was still going on, but he ignored it. The two men who had brought me here still stood behind me. They weren't saying anything and apparently they weren't moving. I couldn't see them, but I knew they were there.

"All right, Curran," Pettit said after a long silence, "I'll tell you how it is. Morgan murdered my son. There is no question whatever about his guilt. I don't want the law messing in this and I don't want you or the *News* messing with it, either. I aim to kill Morgan myself. I don't know where he is, but I've hired a detective agency in Denver to locate him. When they do, I'll go to wherever he is and I will kill him. You go back to Denver and write that. Understand? Morgan is as guilty as hell."

"I understand," I said, "but there's one thing you ought to know. Hank De Bussy and his men are not detectives. They're a bunch of thugs. I know because I've covered stories in Denver and I know how they perform. You'll never see Gordy Morgan. They'll kill him when they find him."

His face darkened and I thought it turned cruel. Maybe it had held that expression all the time, but I hadn't been aware of it until that moment. He said, "I won't pay him if that happens. Gordy Morgan belongs to me. He murdered my son, my only heir. Can you understand?" His hands clenched at his sides. "I will kill him myself. I'll kill him with my own hands. It's the only thing I have left to live for."

"I savvy," I said.

I understood something else, too, as I studied his face. He was a sick man, a crazy man, and therefore more dangerous than a sane man who was basically evil. In that moment I had one of those flashes of the future that come to me occasionally. I sensed, as I stared at his face and his eyes that had become wild and strange, that the evil would not be directed just to Gordy Morgan but to others as well. I knew, then, I would be lucky to get back to Lark alive.

"I don't want you or the law getting into this because you will only muddy the waters," he said, his voice shrill. "It will be hard enough to find him as it is."

"Zach Wheeler says he's in Mexico," I said.

I knew as soon as I said it that I should have kept my mouth shut, but the words were out by that time.

"He's a liar," Pettit screamed.

He nodded at the men behind me. Before I knew

what was happening they had each grabbed a wrist and twisted my arms so that my hands were behind me. Then Pettit hit me in the soft part of the belly. I was unprepared for the blow. The air gushed out of my lungs. My knees turned to rubber and I sagged in the hands of the men who were holding me. I had never felt such agony in my life. It was as if I was choking to death. He hit me again. To me the blows had the power of a mule kick.

The men let me go and I fell into the dust. I fought for breath and I suppose I sucked some into my lungs, but I felt as if my body was paralyzed and I wasn't breathing at all. I lay there, writhing and twisting on the ground. I was vaguely aware of Pettit's words, "If you ain't out of town by morning, I'll kill you. Get him on his horse, boys."

I was lifted into my saddle and the reins were handed to me. I guess I held them. I don't really remember what happened then. The horse started to move. I leaned over the horn. I must have gripped it, although I don't think I had the strength to grip anything very firmly. I guess the racket at the corral was still going on, but I didn't hear it. All that I knew for sure is that the horse got me back to town and somewhere along the way I began to feel that I was breathing again.

CHAPTER XI

My memory is a little fuzzy about what happened after I got back to Lark. I'm sure I paid the liveryman, then I walked to the saloon, leading my horse. I tied him in front, then painfully climbed the stairs to my room and lay down for a while. I had the feeling that the liveryman and bartender both looked at me in surprise as if not expecting me to come back alive, but, as I said, my memory is fuzzy and it may be that I only imagined it.

The one certain memory I have for that afternoon is that my belly was sore as a boil. I didn't have much trouble breathing except for the soreness, but I was worried that I had a serious injury, that something inside me had been knocked loose or broken open.

I hadn't eaten dinner, but I wasn't hungry now and I was sure I couldn't keep anything down if I did eat. Late in the afternoon I rose, got the few things together that I had brought, and went back down the stairs. I certainly wasn't going to let Saul Pettit find me in Lark the next morning.

I paid the saloon man, said I didn't want anything to eat when he asked me, and went outside. I tied my war bag behind the saddle, jammed the Winchester into the boot, and led my horse across the street to the store.

It hurt to walk, but it was less painful than climbing into the saddle and riding. When I got inside the store, I sat down on a pile of sugar sacks. Wheeler came toward me, his face showing his concern. He asked, "What happened?"

I told him, then I said, "They didn't give me a chance to fight. When a man pounds another man who is being held by two other men, I guess it says something about the man who is doing the pounding."

Wheeler nodded. "It does. Pettit's that way. He's a careful man who doesn't take chances. That's how he got to where he is." He scratched his chin, eyeing me. Then he said, "Want to swear out a complaint?"

"No, it wouldn't do any good," I answered. "It would be suicide for you and me to go out there and try to arrest Pettit when he's got a dozen or fifteen cowboys around him. They'd kill us."

"I reckon they would," he agreed. "The trick would be to go when his men are out on the range. They are most of the time. Usually it's just Pettit and his chore boy and the Chinese cook who are at the ranch. They wouldn't give us no trouble."

"What would we do with him after we arrested him?"

"Take him to Trinidad and turn him over to the sheriff."

"On what charge?"

"Assault and battery."

"Oh hell," I said. "Wheeler, do you really want to commit suicide? In the first place we'd never get him to Trinidad. In the second place a jury would never convict him. In the third place, he'd get a hundred-dollar fine and ten days in jail if he was convicted. It isn't worth the risk and you know it."

"Yeah, I reckon you're right," he said regretfully. "The trouble is he does stunts like this and nobody ever picks it up. He knows damned well he can thumb his nose at the law and stay free as a bird."

"I think you really want to try it," I said.

"I do," he said. "Not that I want to die any more than any other man, but I'm getting tired of wearing a star and being so damned helpless."

I thought about what he had said for a while. I knew how he felt, but as far as I was concerned, I had no desire to die from bravery, particularly when there wasn't a chance of succeeding.

"I've got a hunch," I said, "that when this is all over, Saul Pettit is going to get what's coming to him in one way or another, and it won't be over an assault and battery charge. He sure made it clear that he personally was going to kill Gordy—a sort of execution, I guess. That's what will beat him. No man can do that."

"I hope you're right," Wheeler sighed. "Well, what are you going to do now?"

"I'm going up on the mesa," I answered. "Put

some bacon and flour in a sack. Some coffee. A pot and a couple of tin cups. I'm going camping for a day or two."

"You're still crazy," he said, "but it will get you out of Lark."

He brought the sack to me in a few minutes and I paid him, then I asked, "Are there any camping places I can find on the mesa between now and dark?"

He nodded. "There's a good spring beside the trail that you'll find just beyond the Morgan place. It's purty close to Pete Grimes's cabin. Plenty of pine trees and grass for your horse. You'll get there before dark all right."

I shook hands with him, went outside and tied the sack to the saddle horn, then painfully pulled myself into the saddle. I angled south of town, reached the Morgan place, and picked up the trail just beyond there as Wheeler said I would. It wound up the mesa hill in a series of switchbacks.

When I reached the top, I stopped to let my horse blow, and looked back to where I had been. Lark seemed to be a toy town. Beyond it the prairie ran on and on into infinity, the slanting rays of the sun throwing a sharp, clear light upon this primordial land. I wondered how much of that land Saul Pettit owned. I also wondered why it was that so often when a man accumulated that kind of money and the power it bought, he wanted more and more and became harder and harder to satisfy.

I turned my horse and rode west, noting that there were only a few scattered pines on the mesa at this point, but on beyond there were so many trees that they formed a dark mass more black than green in the evening light. The trail took a straight course until it reached the timber, then slanted south. A few minutes later I was through the pines and rode into a large, grass-covered meadow.

To the north I saw the willows that marked a spring at the edge of the trees. I rode to it and dismounted. A large, deep pool of clear water was surrounded by brush and tall grass. A small stream trickled to the north. I suppose it was lost somewhere on the dry mesa hill and probably never reached the prairie below.

I offsaddled, watered my horse, and staked him out in the grass that was knee-high on most of the meadow. I had a long drink and found that the water was sweet and cool, then started gathering wood from windfalls in the timber. I had an idea that I might be able to draw someone to me, maybe Pete Grimes. Although I had to admit that it was a pretty slim notion, I might get Grimes to talk to me up here away from the saloon where the bartender was obviously Saul Pettit's man.

As soon as I started a fire, I put the coffee pot on. By that time it was dark, and although the full moon was in a clear sky, my fire was a bright eye in a pool of near darkness. Presently a man appeared out of the timber and came toward me, slowly at first. I sat motionless beside the fire and pretended that I was not aware of him, but I loosened my gun in the holster and kept my right hand close to the butt.

The man was about fifty yards from me when he called, "Hello."

"Come on in," I called back, "and have a cup of coffee."

He did, still moving slowly as if not certain who I was or why I was there. I saw that it was Grimes before he reached the fire, but I don't think he recognized me until I looked at him and motioned to a tin cup on the ground beside the coffee pot.

"Help yourself, Mr. Grimes," I said.

"I ain't Mr. Grimes to nobody. I'm just Pete." He picked up the cup and poured coffee into it, eyeing me as he did it. Finally he said, "You're the jasper who wanted to talk about Gordy Morgan. Why are you up here and what do you want?"

"I'm up here because Saul Pettit told me he'd kill me if I was in Lark tomorrow morning," I said. "My name is Curt Curran and I'm a reporter for the *Rocky Mountain News.* I was sent down here from Denver to get Gordy Morgan's true story."

For a few seconds I thought he was going to take off again the way he had in the saloon, but he didn't. He finished his coffee and set the cup down, then got his pipe out and filled it. All the time he was sizing me up.

"What side are you on?" he asked.

"I wouldn't be run out of town if I was on Pettit's side," I said. "The more I hear about Gordy, the more I'm inclined to think he was justified in killing the men he did."

"He was." Grimes nodded. "I sure wasn't gonna say that about him down there in Lark, especially in front of that damned bartender. He's a tattler. I knew that if I said anything, it'd get back to Pettit in a hurry and I've had enough trouble with him and his hardcases."

I told him about being taken out to the Rafter P and what had happened, then I added, "You see I've got no reason to be on his side. I'll write the story when I get back to Trinidad, and I'll make Pettit look like the outlaw he is. The trouble is there's still a few pieces missing."

He picked up a flaming twig from the fire, lit his pipe, and puffed for a minute or more, then he said, "I can give you one of the missing pieces, but if you ever tell anybody I was the one who told you, I'll say you are a damned liar."

"Fair enough," I said. "A good reporter never reveals his sources."

"I don't know where Gordy is or where he went after he left here," Grimes said. "Now I ain't told nobody else what I'm gonna tell you, but I'll tell you if it'll help pound a nail into Pettit's coffin. I reckon the *News* ain't read much around here, but the story will get around."

He stopped and puffed on his pipe, still staring at me as if he wanted to be sure his judgment of me was correct. I took a card from my pocket and handed it to him. I said, "Here's my card. It'll help establish my identity."

"I can't read," he mumbled, and threw the card in the fire. "I'll gamble that you're who you say you are. You see, Gordy came up here after he shot Bud. He didn't know for sure he'd killed the bastard, but he knew he'd hit him hard. Also he had a bad hole in his left arm. It was bleeding bad and hurting like hell, but the bullet missed the bone, so it was a matter of wrapping it up and giving him a place to hide while it healed up. He stayed here almost two weeks, then he took off for Trinidad. He didn't aim to stay there. Just buy some grub and then he was gonna keep on riding. I ain't heard from him since."

"A couple of things surprised me," I said. "Why did he trust you?"

"Me and his daddy were good friends," Grimes said gravely. "The best friend I ever had. He'd get a bottle and come up here and we'd sit up and drink and talk all night. Gordy knew that. He knowed I'd never sell him out."

"The second is why didn't Pettit's men find him," I said. "They must have hunted for him."

"They sure did." Grimes slapped his leg and

guffawed. "I hid Gordy out and they didn't find him. That's it in a nutshell. You see, we're close to the New Mexico line. In the old days there was a lot of border hopping. Men who were wanted in the territory came over here and the other way around. I ain't gonna tell you how I done it, but I put one over on Saul Pettit. I've got a cabin that was used for a hide-out for men who were on the dodge. Gordy was safer than he would have been anywhere else, so he stayed till his arm was about healed."

I nodded, knowing he had good reason not to tell me how he had hidden Gordy. I said, "You sure he didn't give you any idea where he was headed?"

Grimes shook his head. "Nope. Fact is, I don't think he knew hisself."

We talked some more. I told Grimes I was staying there for a day or two. I was pretty well stoved up and I didn't feel like riding. He shook his head at me. "You'd better ride in the morning and you'd better start early. They'll kill you if they find you, and you can be damned sure they'll be looking for you."

I didn't argue, but after he left I rolled up in my blanket beside the fire and told myself that Grimes was making too much of it. Pettit had told me to get out of Lark and I had done that. This was a good camping place. I would stay.

CHAPTER XII

Much to my surprise I slept well. I didn't wake up until after the sun was up, and then I lay there for a while, quite comfortable if I didn't move. Suddenly I realized I was hungry. I hadn't eaten since the previous morning. My belly was still sore, and I had trouble breathing if I took a long breath, but I felt better than I had expected.

I rose, built a fire, and put the coffee pot on. I didn't shave, thinking I might be two or three days getting to Trinidad, so I might as well wait until I got there. I had no reason to be concerned about my appearance as long as I was camping.

My surroundings were peaceful. A blue jay made his ugly chatter back in the timber. A squirrel darted along the trunk of a deadfall tree, stopped and stared at me, then disappeared wit a flick of his tail. Several whitefaces appeared in the meadow and began to graze. I was too far away to see the brand, but I guessed they were Rafter P stock unless some of the Morgan stock had escaped being branded by Pettit, and I considered that unlikely.

I fried bacon and opened a can of beans and drank three cups of coffee. It tasted fine. I'd stay here a couple of days, I told myself. It was a pleasure to be here alone although I half expected Pete Grimes to show up and urge me to start riding. He wasn't the most brilliant conversationalist in the world, but I could stand him. He was a decent human being, and after my experience with the Pettit bunch, just being a decent human being placed a man pretty high on my list.

I sat there hunkered by the fire debating about pouring a fourth cup of coffee. For the first time in many days I felt at peace. I refused to think about Gordy Morgan or how much I hated Saul Pettit. My story could wait until I got to Trinidad. I sensed no pressure, I had no ambition, and I began to question my way of life.

I was leading a rat race often filled with danger, no wife, no children, no roots down anywhere. When I reached the end of the trail what would I have? I didn't really like city life. As I thought back over the years, I realized that my happiest time had been when I was growing up on a ranch east of Fort Collins.

I remembered thinking when I got back from Casper that I liked what I was doing and I always swallowed my pride instead of arguing with the Great Man because I liked what I was doing and I didn't want to get fired. But at that exact moment I just didn't give a damn whether I got fired or not.

Then, in spite of myself, I began to think about

Gordy Morgan and wondered where he was and what he was doing. I had felt myself on his side almost from the beginning, maybe because the Great Man back in Denver had sent me on this trip to prove that Gordy Morgan was not the Trouble Kid that the Trinidad *Tribune* had made him out to be.

The more I had dug into the story, the more my sympathies were with the boy, and now after being slugged in Trinidad and beaten by Saul Pettit, my feelings were that of a fanatic. I was going to enjoy writing the story because I had plenty of ammunition to burn Pettit's ass pretty well.

Now that I thought about it, I wanted to do more. I had considered returning to Denver and telling the Great Man I had lost track of Gordy, that if Pettit's detectives couldn't turn him up, I didn't have much chance of doing it, but now I found my feelings doing a complete reversal. I wasn't at peace with myself now and I wouldn't be until I found and talked with Gordy Morgan.

Suddenly I was aware that two riders had emerged from the timber to the east. I assumed they were Rafter P hands. I got up and moved back toward the trees where I had leaned my rifle against a pine trunk. Now I wished I had taken Grimes's advice and ridden out before sunup. At the moment I didn't have any reason to be scared, but the intrusion of the men broke my line of thought. Anyway I looked at it, I couldn't see any Rafter P men being friendly.

Apparently the men didn't see me until they were almost opposite me. My fire had burned down, I was standing in the shadow of the pines, and my horse was grazing quietly, so there had been nothing to attract their attention. If I had pulled back into the timber, they might have ridden by and nothing would have happened, but one of them glanced in my direction and saw me.

For a moment the man stared, then he let out a whoop and yelled, "There he is, Curly. Let's get him."

They turned their horses toward me, dug in the steel, and came straight at me. They hadn't traveled more than ten feet before they pulled their guns and started shooting. Now I have had a lot of things happen to me that scared hell out of me, but I had never been shot at before, and it made a mighty strange sensation in my guts that had nothing to do with the soreness that had been there.

I had sense enough to drop to my knees so I'd make a smaller target. I grabbed the Winchester, levered a shell into the chamber, and started shooting. My first shot was a complete miss and I understood what Wheeler had said about hitting a man on a running horse. These men were covering ground fast, and I had a terrible feeling they were going to be on me before I got them.

The bullets were coming too close for me to be comfortable. One of them struck the tree I was hugging and showered me with bits of bark. Another bored a hole through the top of my hat and a third caught my left shoulder, making a red welt across the top of my collar bone.

My second shot knocked the lead man out of his saddle, but my third was a miss. The remaining man was close now and I had a crazy feeling he'd just pull his horse to a stop and fire down at me from about five feet away and I'd be a dead man.

It didn't happen that way and the only reason it didn't was that someone started shooting from the timber a short distance to the west. The rider threw up his hands and spilled out of his saddle in a rolling fall that brought him to the edge of my fire. The horse turned and ran off along the edge of the timber.

"You all right?" a man yelled.

It was Pete Grimes's voice. I was sure of that. I sat down, my Winchester between my legs, my knees like rubber. I guess that half a minute went by before I could find my voice and call back, "I'm all right."

I still hadn't moved when he appeared, holding his rifle at the ready, his gaze pinned on the fallen men. He went to them and rolled them over on their backs. "You got lucky on your first shot," he said. "Right in the brisket. These jaspers won't be giving us no more trouble." He turned and looked at me as he said truculently, "You didn't believe me last night, did you?"

"No, I didn't," I admitted. "It just didn't seem reasonable that Pettit would try to have me killed after I did what he told me to."

"He loves to man-hunt," Grimes said sourly. "He's like a cat with a mouse. He'll tell his man to leave, then he'll turn his hounds loose. I guess they kill just for the fun of killing."

"You were sure in the right place at the right time," I said. "How long had you been there?"

"All night," he said.

"My God," I said. "I didn't expect anything like that. I'd have been a dead man if you hadn't been looking out for me."

"That you would," he agreed.

I managed to get to my feet and shook his hand. He didn't look like the poverty-stricken old hermit who had been cadging drinks in the Lark saloon. Instead, to me he was a fine, upstanding man to whom I owed my life.

"I sure can't pay you back," I said. "All I can say is thanks."

"No, you can fry Pettit's ass just like you promised," he said. "That's all I'm asking."

"I'll do it," I said. "I've got enough personal reasons."

He leaned his rifle against a tree trunk. "Now get packed up and start riding," he said. "I'll fetch their horses and we'll send the carcasses back to Pettit. He won't be able to do much until tomorrow morning, and by that time you'd better be in Trinidad."

"I figure on it," I said.

It didn't take me long to saddle up, tie my sack of grub to the horn, kick out what was left of the fire, and help Grimes lift the dead men into their saddles and watch him lash them into place. He took off the horses' bridles and gave each a clout across the rump.

He turned to me. "Get moving," he said. "Pettit's going to ride up here and ask me what happened. I'll tell him you got both of 'em."

"Sure." I took a ten-dollar gold piece from my pocket and gave it to him. "Have a few drinks in the saloon and surprise the bartender by paying for them."

He took the money, a slow grin spreading across his face. "That I will, Mr. Curran, that I will."

I stepped into the saddle and rode away. I turned and waved once and he waved back. A moment later I was lost in the timber. The thought occurred to me as I rode through the cool shade that you never can tell by looking at a frog how far he can jump, and you can't tell by looking at a man what he'll do in the crunch. I was alive because my first impression of Pete Grimes had been dead wrong.

CHAPTER XIII

I reached Trinidad late in the afternoon, returned my horse to the livery stable and paid my bill, then walked to the Columbian Hotel. I signed the register, retrieved my suitcase, and went up the stairs to my room. I thought about seeing the sheriff, but decided he had gone home by this time, so I had supper in the dining room instead, thinking that tomorrow would be time enough to see Garcia.

When I walked past the desk on the way back to my room, I saw that the night clerk had come on duty. I stopped and asked, "Were you working the night a man was killed upstairs? About five or six weeks ago?"

He nodded. "I sure was. I hope we don't have any more killings here. A murdered man is a hell of a thing to find in a room."

"Tell me about it."

He stared at me a moment as if trying to figure out why I was pumping him, then he shrugged. "I was right here at the desk when I heard the shooting. I knew it came from upstairs. It was purty early. Not much later than this. I ran up the stairs and found the door of Room 22 ajar. I went in and here was the man's body lying on the floor. He'd been shot in the chest. He was dead as near as I could tell. People began crowding in. I asked one man to go for the law and another one to get a doctor. They had both been living here for a couple of months so they knew where to go.

"I thought at first it was suicide. There was a gun on the floor beside him but there wasn't no powder burns on him; then I saw that the window was open. I went over to it and looked out, but it was dark then and I couldn't see anybody. The roof of Doc Miggs's drug store is just below the window. I had a notion the killer had dropped to the roof and ran. I didn't see anybody in the hall when I came up the stairs, so I know he didn't leave by the back stairs."

"You didn't know the murdered man?"

The clerk shook his head. "He wasn't anybody staying here. As far as I know, he ain't ever been identified."

"But you're sure he wasn't the man who had rented the room?"

"Sure I'm sure," he said indignantly. "I know the man who rented the room. He had registered the night before. Signed his name John Smith from Denver."

"You remember what he looked like?"

"Yeah, I do. He was a handsome young buck, the kind you remember. I admit that a lot of men go through here that I couldn't tell you a thing about them a week later, but I remember this one. He was redheaded and had two, three weeks growth of red whiskers on his face. Blue eyes. Big, maybe six feet tall, and he walked with a limp. Not much, but I remember he limped as he walked across the lobby. I wondered what had given him the limp and that it was too bad because he was a fine broth of a lad in every other way."

"You figure he killed the man that was in his room?"

The clerk nodded. "I sure do. I had seen him cross the lobby just a little while before that, going to his room, and I hadn't seen anybody else go up the stairs, though I reckon that don't prove anything. Besides, he didn't have no luggage, so I made him pay when he registered. He signed up for three days and he was here only one. Now that don't happen very often. He just plain disappeared. I guess the sheriff and the police looked for him, but he'd taken his horse from the livery stable. By the time they were looking for him in daylight, he was a long ways from here. Probably rode across Raton Pass and went south."

"Probably." I took Gordy's picture from my pocket and showed it to him. "That him?"

The clerk studied the picture for a long time. Finally he said, "Well sir, I ain't sure. I think it is, but you know, you put the start of a red beard on a face and it changes him. I think it's him, though. Who is he?"

"The man I'm looking for, John Smith," I said. "What livery stable did he leave his horse in?"

"Barney Brady's," he answered. "About a block down the street. Say, you don't think his name really is John Smith, do you?"

"There are a lot of John Smiths in the world," I said. "Thanks for the information."

I went up the stairs to my room, and this time I moved through the door cautiously, my gun in my hand. I didn't know if De Bussy's men were still around or not, but I wasn't taking any chances. I didn't know, either, if they would jump me again if they were in town—because they wouldn't know whether I had given up working on the Morgan case or not. But I was sure of one thing. When Saul Pettit failed to find me on the mesa, he would alert De Bussy's detectives and they'd be on my tail for sure. I figured I had about two days. When they were up, I'd be out of town.

I spent a couple of hours that evening working on my story and I had it finished by the tag end of the following afternoon. I had brought several manila envelopes in my suitcase. I got one out, addressed it to the Great Man at the *Rocky Mountain News*, slipped my story into it along with a personal note I had written, and sealed it. I knew the Great Man would work my story over, probably taming down some of the tough phrases I had used.

I had indeed fried Saul Pettit's ass and any reader would wonder why the man was not in jail. None of my copy ever got into the columns of the newspaper exactly the way I wrote it, which always irritated me, but I finally quit reading what appeared in print because I figured there wasn't any use to object.

With a few words the Great Man could slant a story the way he wanted it, and he was the boss. This time I was sure he wanted Gordy Morgan to appear innocent, but he wouldn't be anxious to risk a libel suit just to make Pettit look bad. Anyhow, I had done all I could to keep my promise to Pete Grimes.

In my personal note I said I'd try to pick up Gordy Morgan's trail, but, as of now, I didn't know where to look. I clapped my hat on my head and, leaving the hotel, walked to the post office and mailed the envelope. I suddenly felt a great relief because I'd had a lingering fear that Pettit through De Bussy could somehow prevent my writing and mailing the story. Now it was out of Pettit's control.

I stopped at Brady's livery stable and asked him if he remembered a man or men who had left a horse or horses here the night the man was killed in the Columbian Hotel. At first he said no, that it was too long ago and he couldn't remember all the saddle bums who stopped and left horses overnight, but after I gave him the description the hotel clerk had given me, he nodded and said he did remember that man. Then I asked if he remembered the horse.

The liveryman had been cleaning out a stall. Now he leaned against the wall of the stall and scratched the back of his neck. Finally he said, "Yeah, I think I do. I remember him because he was a fine looking gelding. After seeing some of the broomtails that come in here, you look twice at a horse like that one. He was a bay, big and leggy. Had four white stockings and a star on his forehead if I'm remembering the right animal. I mean, I ain't real sure I've got the right man hooked up with the right horse, but I think that's the way it was."

I thanked him and left the stable. I turned toward the courthouse, thinking that I really hadn't needed the liveryman's testimony, but it nailed down my suspicions that the killer in the hotel room was Gordy Morgan. I still had no evidence as to why the dead man was in Gordy's room or who he was or why Gordy had killed him. I could only guess.

I caught the sheriff before he left the office. I think he was surprised to see me. He motioned me to a chair as he said, "I've been wondering how you made out in Lark. I had a hunch you'd have trouble, so I'm glad to see you alive."

"With no thanks to Saul Pettit," I said.

I told him what had happened, ending up by showing him the hole in the crown of my hat and the hole in my shirt. I said, "I'm lucky that slug didn't come a little lower. As it is, I've just got a red welt that looks like I've had a hot branding iron on my tender hide."

Garcia shook his head. "I can't protect you, Curran. I told you that. I hope you'll be on the next train to Denver."

"No, I won't be on that train," I said. "I remember what you told me. I just couldn't believe that Pettit was the madman you made him out to be."

"You know now," he said. "What are you going to do?"

"I don't know, but I'm into this thing to the finish. I told myself that before, but I don't know that I really meant it until Pettit sent those gun-slicks after me. I aim to really fry him. The trouble is, I don't know where to look for Gordy."

"I can't help you on that," he said. "I've looked for him more than I told you, and I've sent word to sheriffs in New Mexico to be on the lookout for him. So far I've heard absolutely nothing. Sometimes I wonder if he's hid out around here."

He tapped his finger tips on the desk top, his gaze on the far wall. "Curran, you want to swear out a warrant for Pettit's arrest? You've certainly got assault and battery for a charge, and maybe attempted murder if Pete Grimes will testify. He hates Pettit enough to do it."

I had a feeling about Garcia just as I'd had with Wheeler that he really wanted to try it, that he'd like nothing better than to throw Pettit into jail, but I shook my head. "We'd never get him here,"

I said, "and if we did, he'd never be convicted. No, I want to talk to Gordy. I'll know what to do then. Anyhow, I've got a funny feeling about this. I think that when a man is possessed the way Pettit is, he's going to overreach himself and wind up cutting his own throat."

Garcia shrugged. "The question is whether you'll live long enough to find Gordy. Pettit may come in and charge you with murdering his two boys."

"What will you say to that?"

"I'll say that I have to have more evidence than he's got before I make an arrest, but if I'm beaten in this fall's election, you may be in trouble."

"That'll be a while yet." I leaned forward and fixed my gaze on Garcia's face. "You've known all the time that the fellow who killed the man in the Columbian Hotel was Gordy, haven't you?"

That startled him. He said, "You guessed it before. Now you sound as if you're sure."

"I'm sure," I said, "but I don't know why he killed him."

"We can make a good guess," Garcia said. "It probably was one of De Bussy's men who recognized Gordy and tried to take him to Pettit. Gordy knew Pettit would murder him if he let that happen, so he managed to kill the fellow. I don't know how, but Gordy's lucky and he's a fighter, and when you put those together, you've got a man who is probably going to survive."

"If you've known it was Gordy, why haven't you made a serious effort to bring him in?" I asked.

"I have, damn it," he said sharply. "I just got done telling you that. I didn't look very hard for him after the Lark killings, but this time I figured I'd better hear his side of it. Well, he's gone, just plumb vanished."

I rose. I didn't know what else to say. I had felt all the time that Garcia wanted Saul Pettit's hide a lot more than he wanted Gordy Morgan's. Perhaps it was a matter of keeping his job. He may very well have figured that there were more people in the county who hated Pettit than who wanted to see Gordy tried, that the *Tribune* hadn't aroused as much public sentiment as would be expected.

"I'll keep in touch with you," I said, and left the office.

I stopped in the hotel dining room and had supper, then stepped into the bar and had a drink. I kept trying to figure out my next move, but I couldn't see a move to make. Garcia had tried to find Gordy and had failed. He certainly had more connections than I had, so what chance did I have to find Gordy, particularly after so much time had passed?

By the time I went upstairs to my room, it was dark. When I reached the dimly lighted hall, I stopped, my heart skipping a few beats. The door to my room was open and the light was on. I drew my gun, certain that whoever was in my room had no business being there and was not a friend.

I tiptoed toward the door, my cocked gun in my hand. I eased along the wall opposite the door until I could see inside. There was Hank De Bussy sitting in a chair by the window on the far side of the room, a long cigar in his mouth.

I stood there for a long moment, staring at him, too astonished to move. He was the last man I expected to see, and, next to Saul Pettit, the last man I wanted to see.

CHAPTER XIV

I moved across the hall and into the room, my gun covering De Bussy. I asked, "What are you doing here?"

"Come in and close the door," he said. "I thought it was about time for you to show up."

"The door stays open," I said. "What are you doing here?"

"I came to talk," he said. "I've got a proposition to offer you."

"I don't want to have anything to do with you, De Bussy," I said. "I know exactly what you are and none of it's good. There's no proposition you can offer me that would interest me, not after one of your men knocked me cold a few nights ago."

"I apologize for my man's zeal," he said. "I am indeed sorry about that, but you see, Mr. Pettit hired us with definite orders to find Gordy Morgan and not to be influenced by other parties. We were to discourage them because he wanted the personal satisfaction of dealing with Gordy Morgan. This was before you or the *Rocky Mountain News* was involved in the case. What he was most interested in was keeping the law from scaring Morgan out of the country. If he is in the United States, we'll run him down sooner or later."

"Why didn't he cool the *Tribune* off if he didn't want to scare Gordy?" I demanded.

He shrugged. "I'm a logical man, Curran. So are you. Saul Pettit isn't. The only answer I can give you is that he aims to kill Morgan, and he figured that the *Tribune* would work up enough public sentiment against Morgan so that he'd be in the clear after he finished the boy. You know, the wronged father exacting justice after the law had failed."

It made sense in a roundabout sort of way, I thought. I motioned to the door. "All right, we've talked. Now get out."

"Not till I've given you my proposition," he said. "Put your gun away. You're not going to use it. I'm unarmed. You wouldn't shoot an unarmed man."

I sat down on the bed and stared at De Bussy. He was right. He knew me pretty well and I thought I knew him. I had known him for a number of years and had covered several cases that involved him and Soapy Smith before Smith left for Alaska.

He was a brutal man with little of Smith's smoothness and cleverness. Together they had made a good team running Denver's underworld, but after he was alone, he went downhill pretty fast, proving that as far as he was concerned crime didn't pay. That was probably the reason he had started his detective agency. I don't know how well he was doing, but he'd been at it for a year or more, so he must be making money.

He was a grotesque looking man, about six feet tall with a bulging belly, almost no neck, and a head that was absolutely bald. I'd guess he weighed about two hundred and fifty pounds. He was very strong for all of his belly. I'd watched him in barroom brawls and I'd seen him take an amazing amount of punishment, but he'd always given more than he received.

He had a bushy, black mustache, a massive chin, and a badly pocked face that made him look like a walking nightmare. Actually he *was* a nightmare. If he had anything that resembled a conscience, I had never detected it.

"I told Pettit that you didn't have a detective agency," I said. "I told him you were a bunch of thugs."

"Quite right," he agreed, smiling. "I would say

that pleased him because that's exactly what he wants. Now then, are you ready to listen?"

"You're wasting your breath," I said, "but I'll listen if you will get out of here as soon as you're finished."

"I'll be glad to," he said. "I have no more love for you than you have for me. Your lousy rag has been after me for years, but you've never nailed me to the wall and never will. The only reason I've been sitting here waiting for you is that it occurred to me that we were after the same thing and we might be of help to each other. Not because we like each other, mind you. It's just that we have a common objective."

"When I hear you talk," I said, "I always get the feeling that you are an educated man. Funny that your education never gave you a sense of morals."

"Morals handicap a man," he said genially. "I was never infected. Now, as I was saying, we have a common objective. I want to find Gordy Morgan to get my fee. You want to find him to get your story. My proposition is that we exchange any information that we have which might be beneficial in finding the boy."

"I told Pettit that you'd kill him when you found him," I said. "If that happens, I'd never get my story."

"What did Pettit say to that?" he asked.

"He said he wouldn't pay you if you did."

He laughed softly. "And I want to be paid. No,

I will not kill the boy unless he forces it. I intend to find him and hold him while I send word to Pettit that I have him. Now what do you know that would interest me?"

I must have sat there a full minute studying the big man as I mentally weighed the pros and cons of trying to bargain with a man like him, a man without morals or principles of any kind unless it could be called a principle to do anything that would make a dollar.

Actually I didn't know anything that would help find Gordy and I wouldn't have told De Bussy if I had, but it was possible he'd tell me something that would be useful. As it stood now, I was up against a blank wall, so anything he said might help.

"All right," I said, "it's a deal if I have your word that I will have a chance to talk to young Morgan."

"You have my word," he said, "if I know where to find you."

I didn't think his word meant anything, but I thought he expected it and he might believe me when I told him I had only one thing to tell him. I said, "I'm not sure this has anything to do with finding Gordy, and it's all that I know that you don't know. He was wounded in the shoot-out with Bud. He stayed on the mesa for a couple of weeks before he rode into Trinidad."

"I'll be damned," he said softly. "You sure?"

"I wasn't there," I said, "so I can't be sure of my own knowledge, but I'm as sure as I can be of anything I've been told."

He took the cigar out of his mouth and rolled it between his fingers thoughtfully. "I don't savvy that," he said. "Pettit told me he used a fine-toothed comb on the mesa, but I've wondered where Gordy was between the business in Lark and his killing my man here in this hotel. I just can't explain Pettit missing him."

"He knew the mesa," I said. "He must have found a cave or somewhere to hide. Anyhow, he apparently came into town when his wound healed enough for him to ride."

"It makes sense that way," De Bussy agreed. "We kept thinking that he'd lit out for Mexico, but he didn't. All right, I'll tell you what I know, which is exactly nothing, but I can tell you what he didn't do. He wouldn't have circled back and gone east because there was too much chance that Pettit's men would pick him up, so I sent my men south across Raton Pass to look for him. Nobody saw or heard anything of him. I have good connections in New Mexico. He'd have been seen somewhere in a saloon, a livery stable, a ranch, a hotel or a store. He could have traveled at night and gone a ways, but sooner or later he would have stopped for grub or a drink or to trade horses if he was moving fast."

"Maybe people lied to your men," I said.

"Nobody lied to Hank De Bussy," he said. "They know better. Besides, why would they? None of them would have owed Morgan anything and we were offering money for any kind of a lead that held up."

"Then he headed north," I said. "Maybe to Denver. The best place to hide out is a city. You know that."

"Sure I know that," he agreed, "but he's a country boy. He would be lost in a city. You've got to know cities to hide out in them. He'd be a lamb among wolves. Anyhow, I sent my men north after we drew a blank in New Mexico. We had the same thing north. No, he didn't go that way, either. At least I'm convinced he didn't."

"That leaves two alternatives," I said. "He might be hiding out here in Trinidad."

"Then why did he come to the hotel if he had a place to hide out?" he asked. "Besides, I've been informed that he had practically never left Lark in his life and that he had no friends here."

"That agrees with what I was told," I said. "That leaves only one other possibility. He went west."

"Up the Picketwire," De Bussy shook his head. "We checked that, too. Nobody up there saw him. He might have made it into the mountains without being seen, I guess, but again, he's not a mountain man and you have to know the mountains to live in them. Anyhow, he'd have to buy grub. After killing my man in the hotel, he was in a hurry getting out of town. What's he living on?"

I threw up my hands. "He's disappeared into thin air."

"Naw, he's got to be somewhere." De Bussy rose. "I guess our conversation was an exercise in futility." He walked to the door, then stopped and looked back. "You ready to give up and go back to Denver?"

Right then I saw what he had been up to. He wanted me out of the way and if he made my job look impossible, I'd quit. I said, "Maybe I am. It looks impossible."

"That it does," he said, and left the room.

I lay awake a long time that night thinking what Garcia had said, and then about what De Bussy had told me. I figured Garcia had quit looking, but De Bussy hadn't. He hadn't given me any kind of a notion as to where he would look now or what he would do, but he wouldn't quit as long as Pettit was paying, and as possessed as Pettit was with finding and killing Gordy, he'd keep on paying.

Remembering that I had brought a map of Colorado with me, I got out of bed, rummaged around in my suitcase until I found the map, and studied it. I thought of the possibility that Gordy might have gone as far north as Walsenburg and then headed across La Veta Pass and in San Luis Valley. If he had, he might be anywhere now.

I kept coming back to the Picketwire, the

thought nagging me that Gordy didn't want to go so far that he couldn't get back when he wanted to. I'd had the conviction all along that Gordy planned to return someday to Lark and settle with Saul Pettit.

I put the map back into the suitcase and went to bed. When I woke up in the morning, I had made up my mind. I'd ride up the Picketwire. It was as good a place as any to look for Gordy. Or maybe my decision stemmed from desperation because I didn't know where else to look. Anyhow, I had one of my hunches that I'd find Gordy somewhere west of Trinidad.

CHAPTER XV

I woke early the following morning, got up and shaved, and went downstairs for breakfast. I returned to my room and packed my suitcase, leaving a few things such as my shaving gear to carry in my war bag. I paid my bill, asked again for permission to store my suitcase, and left the hotel.

I walked rapidly to the livery stable, my Winchester in my right hand, and was fortunate in being able to rent the same horse I had used previously. He was a big roan, no beauty and no racer, but I was comfortable with him. I had been raised on a ranch a few miles east of Fort Collins, so I'd had plenty of experience with horses. Too, I'd used them many times since I'd started working for the *News*, but I didn't consider myself an expert with horses and I had no desire to prove myself a buckaroo when I started out in the morning.

I followed the Picketwire for two days, stopping in every town I passed through and at every ranch I saw and asking if anyone had seen a man within the last few weeks who answered Gordy's description. I showed my picture of him, but the answer was always no. If he had gone through here, he must have traveled at night as De Bussy had suggested.

Near the end of the second day the Stone Wall began looming up ahead of me. I had heard about it, but it surpassed anything I had heard. It was exactly what the name implied, a stone wall lifting three or four hundred feet above the relatively level floor of the valley.

With a little imagination a man might see the wall as the work of an ancient tribe of giants who had inhabited this land in prehistoric times. The wall was composed of red rock, but it didn't really give a red appearance because it was partly covered by green and yellow moss. The wall varied in height, giving a sort of stairstep effect as if built of blocks of irregular shape. Here and there small pines grew out of the top of the wall, with scrub oak along the bottom.

On beyond were the foothills of the Sangre de

Cristo range, then beyond them were the high mountains: great, granite peaks that resembled the teeth of a giant saw set hard against a bright, blue sky. Now, in August, there was hardly a trace of snow that was visible to me, just those soaring, savage peaks that formed a barrier to westward travel.

Late in the afternoon I reached the small town of Stonewall that was set among the pines at the foot of the wall. Now that I was close I saw that a road ran through a gap in the wall. If Gordy had come this far, he could have gone on or he could have turned south into New Mexico. He must have stopped here. He didn't know the country; he probably stopped and asked about what lay ahead.

Stonewall was a vacation spot for Trinidad people who came here to fish or hunt, or just to lie in the shade of the pines. It was entirely different country than the brown, almost barren valley through which I had been traveling. The air was cool and sweet, the grass knee high where it hadn't been cut or grazed, and a clear, swift-flowing stream, which would be a fork of the Picketwire, ran through a gap in the wall.

The town wasn't much: a two-story log building which was the hotel, a store, a stable, and a post office, and maybe twenty houses scattered through the trees. I turned into the stable, left my horse with orders for a rubdown and a double bait of oats and, taking my Winchester and war bag, started toward the hotel. I stopped, noticing a rider on a pinto coming toward me.

I had seen that horse a dozen times in the last two days. He had always been behind me, never in front. I hadn't thought about being followed, and certainly not by one of De Bussy's men. I was sure I had convinced him that I didn't know any more about Gordy's whereabouts than he did, but now it struck me that I *had* been followed. His arrival in Stonewall after following me for two days was too much.

I stood at the edge of the road and watched him as he rode up. He was a young man, short and stocky, with a red, sunburned face. He was wearing a brown, broadcloth suit and a derby hat. Obviously he was not a cowboy or a native of this part of the country. He rode slouched in the saddle and his face had a pained expression as if every step his horse took jolted and hurt him.

He disappeared through the archway of the stable. I waited until he came out. He approached me, walking stiffly and making a point of not looking at me as he passed me. I didn't say a word until he had gone by. When he was two steps beyond me, I said, "I'm here, friend."

He turned and looked at me, apparently surprised. He said, "All right, you're here. Is that supposed to mean something?"

"You've been behind me for two days," I said.

"I figured you must have some business with me and couldn't catch me."

"I have no business with you unless you're interested in buying a set of encyclopedias," he said. "I'm selling them. If you have children, you need them. School libraries do not have sufficient books to satisfy the natural curiosity of a child who is in that stage of development in which his natural, inquisitive nature takes over. If this is stifled, you do him irreparable harm. Now why don't we go back into the hotel lobby and I'll show you a prospectus of the . . ."

"All right," I interrupted. "It seems that I guessed wrong. I don't have any children, so I'm not interested. I thought you were tailing me."

He scowled. He was not a pleasant-looking man and I still wasn't convinced he was what he said he was. I couldn't tell whether he was carrying a gun under his coat or not. He seemed to be the kind of man who would work for De Bussy and certainly not a salesman type who would be peddling encyclopedias in this part of the country to poor farmers who were largely Mexicans and who, judging from the small, adobe houses and rundown fields, were having trouble making even a meager living.

Of course I was jumping to conclusions when I decided what he looked like and who he should be working for, and he did have his spiel down pat, but that didn't prove anything. He stood staring at me a moment, his fists clenched as if he was fighting an impulse to take a poke at me, then he shrugged his shoulders and went on into the hotel without another word.

I waited until he was inside the hotel before I followed. I waited while he registered, noting the luxuriant growth of a row of potted geraniums on a table near the window. They had a dozen or more blossoms, a delicate salmon color that I had never seen before. Someone, I thought, had a green thumb. Many hotel lobbies have flowers, but most of the ones I had seen were a sickly yellow-green.

There was a bar on one side of the lobby, a dining room on the other. The smell of cooking food that came from the dining room was enough to make my stomach do flip-flops. My eating since I'd left Trinidad had been mighty thin prairie fare, and I was ravenous.

As soon as the peddler finished registering and took his key, I moved up, leaned my Winchester against the desk, and signed my name. I saw that the peddler had given his name as Jerry Hahn from Denver. I remembered that a man named Hahn had been arrested in Denver several times on bunco charges, but I didn't know him personally. There could be a dozen Hahns in Denver, so I wasn't proving anything.

I laid the pen down and, taking Gordy's picture from my pocket, showed it to the clerk. I asked,

"Have you seen this man go through here within the last six weeks? He's young, about eighteen, and has red hair and probably a short beard. He walks with a slight limp."

The clerk picked a pair of spectacles and put them on. He studied the picture for a long time, then shook his head. "No sir, I ain't seen him. Does the law want him?"

"No, I just want to find him," I said. "Suppose he did ride through here. Would he have been likely to have turned south into New Mexico?"

"Not if he knew what was good for him," the clerk said. "That's the Vermijo Grant south of the line. They're purty hard on trespassers. Of course if he was a stranger, he wouldn't know that, but he'd soon find out once he was across the line. Besides, there's plenty of NO TRESPASSING signs along the road, so if he had any sense, he'd have turned back." He reversed the register and looked at my name. "You gonna be with us very long, Mr. Curran?"

"Just tonight, I think," I said.

As I picked up my rifle and turned from the desk, I saw a boy shuffle along the side of the table that held the geraniums, a watering can in his hand. He was about fifteen, I guessed, with a round, overlarge head and heavy features. He glanced once at the man behind the desk and I saw that his eyes seemed to bulge from his head. His face was blank, holding no expression whatever.

"You have the finest geraniums I ever saw," I said.

"They're doing fine," he agreed. "Larry there tends 'em like a mother. I guess if you love flowers, they love you back and do well."

I'd never heard that before, but maybe it worked that way. At least the boy seemed very concerned about them. I climbed the stairs, wondering about him. I had a feeling he wasn't very bright, but I'd learned a long time ago that I couldn't judge a man's intelligence by his looks.

My room was comfortable and clean which I expected it to be since this was something of a resort hotel. I washed and combed my hair, then went downstairs for supper. They served family style around a long table, and I had to wait a few minutes until all the residents arrived.

The peddler Hahn took a seat at the far end of the table from me. I was agreeable to that as I still had a very uneasy feeling about him. The rest of the crowd was composed of Trinidad people, mostly couples who apparently knew each other and were here simply to do nothing. They kept up a continual flow of talk, and neither Hahn nor I participated except to ask for some item of food.

The meal was excellent, the food ample, the first good meal I'd had in two days. Hahn rose and left the table before I finished my dessert, a large serving of chocolate cake. From the talk, I gathered that the hotel clerk owned the place. He sat at one end of the table, his very fat wife at the other. I got up, complimented the host on the excellent meal, and went outside.

I walked around the hotel wanting to get some exercise, realizing I had eaten too much. I reached the back of the building when the boy Larry stepped out through a rear door and motioned to me. I had no idea what he was up to, so I hesitated, but he kept on motioning, so I walked up to him.

He hugged the wall and kept glancing in both directions as if he didn't want anyone to see him talking to me. He said, "I seen the man you were asking Grandpop about. I'll tell you for ten dollars if you promise you won't tell anybody I told you. I'm not supposed to tell anybody. Grandpop, he promised Judy he wouldn't tell."

I dug a ten-dollar gold piece out of my pocket and gave it to him. He felt of it, bit down on it, and then shoved it into his pants pocket. He said, "He rode through here on a bay horse and stayed one night. It was about six weeks ago, maybe less. I forget for sure how long ago it was. He's working on the BB. That's Judy Bishop's ranch."

He reached behind him to open the back door, his head still turning back and forth to see if anyone was watching. I grabbed his arm, asking, "Have you told anyone else?"

He nodded. "One man. About a week ago. I

told him not to tell nobody. Grandpop would skin me if he knowed I'd told."

I let him go then. He disappeared, closing the door behind him. I walked on through the pine trees, thinking that I'd found Gordy Morgan at last. But who was the other man who had been asking for him? It seemed a good guess that he would be one of Hank De Bussy's crew. If that was true, De Bussy then had known all the time where Gordy was when he was talking to me and he had lied. Another question came into my mind. If De Bussy knew where Pettit could find Gordy, had he informed Pettit, and was Pettit on his way here?

I had no answers, but I told myself I had been right in thinking De Bussy was trying to discourage me and get me started back to Denver. It probably also explained why he had put a man on my tail, wanting to find out why I hadn't gone back to Denver, or at least find out how much I knew about Gordy's whereabouts, and whether I had lied.

I didn't doubt now that Jerry Hahn was indeed De Bussy's man. Well, I'd see more of him, I was sure, but what counted was that I'd see Gordy Morgan, too, and I could wind up my assignment.

CHAPTER XVI

I was later getting away in the morning than I had hoped because no one in the hotel was in a hurry about serving breakfast. As soon as I had eaten, I climbed the stairs to my room, shaved, and went back to the lobby, my war bag in one hand, my Winchester in the other. I paid my bill, deciding not to ask about the location of the BB ranch because I might get the boy Larry into trouble. I did ask when I got my horse at the livery stable.

"North of here a piece," the liveryman said. "Just go through the gap in the wall and follow the road. You'll get there. You'll pass some farms on the other side of the wall, then the road peters out so it ain't much more'n a trail, but stay on it."

I thanked him, mounted, and rode through the gap. He was right about the road. After riding a mile or so, I was out of the farming area and the road began to climb through a thick growth of quakies. They were the biggest quakie trees I had ever seen. I felt as if I had moved into a temple of nature, the road barely wide enough for a wagon, the tree limbs meeting overhead so that the ground was perpetually in shade.

I had a strange feeling, as if I had been transported from all of the fears and turbulence and striving of man into another world of quiet, of peace, of harmony. As I rode, my horse's hoofs dropping silently into the soft earth that was covered by the fallen leaves of the quakies, I felt lifted up and exalted, and I asked myself if I could ever again exist in the boiling pot that was Denver.

The air was cool and damp, and now and then I heard the distant rumble of thunder to the west. A big buck flashed across the road. A startled jay made a streak of blue ahead of me and disappeared into the trees. The ratatat of a woodpecker momentarily shattered the quiet and then it was gone and the silence descended upon me again.

I came out of the quakies as quickly as I had come into them. A ranch lay before me. It was the BB, I thought. I reined up and took it all in with one great gulp, then I began seeing details. Beyond any doubt it was a story-book spread in a big meadow that had to be over one hundred acres. The meadow was surrounded by quakies and pines. A creek ran through the middle, the land sloping gradually toward the stream that ran into a small, reed-bordered pond, then meandered across the rest of the flat to disappear into the quakies.

The one fact that struck me above everything else was the orderliness of the place. Everything was exactly where it should be, the two-story log house, the log barn, the outbuildings, the corrals, the garden back of the house, and the splash of color that a flower bed made across the front of the house.

A field directly ahead of me held a multitude of shocks of hay; a good crop, it seemed to me. On beyond the house on the other side of the creek lay a pasture. A small herd of whitefaces grazed near the edge of the timber. Ahead of me not more than fifty yards away I saw a wagon being loaded with hay.

At first I had an idea that the man loading the wagon was Gordy Morgan. For a moment I had a crazy dread of going up to the man and recognizing Gordy and having this whole mission come to an end. It had been interesting and exciting, and although last night I had looked forward to ending my assignment today, now I perversely didn't want it to end.

The feeling was only a passing impulse. I rode toward the wagon, noting that only one person was working. I had not gone more than twenty feet before I saw that the person ahead of me was a woman, a large, strong woman judging from the way she handled her pitchfork and the shock of hay, but definitely a woman, wearing men's clothes. Being alone, she was doing this the hardest way possible, forking the hay to the wagon and then climbing onto the load and spreading the hay, then driving ahead to the next shock and getting back on the ground again.

Suddenly as I rode toward the wagon, the

realization that my assignment was not about to end here flooded through me. If Gordy Morgan was working for this woman, he'd be out here helping her. I was fully aware then how my feeling of not wanting my assignment to end had indeed been a passing whim. I had been on this job long enough. I wanted to get it over with.

Apparently the woman was not aware of my presence until I was only a few feet from her. She finished with a shock of hay and tossed the fork onto the wagon, then I suppose she heard my horse. Whirling, she saw me and appeared startled.

"Good morning, ma'am," I said. "Are you looking for a hay hand?"

"I certainly am," she said, "but you don't look like a hay hand."

I reined up and stepped down, lifting my hat to her. "Looks are deceiving," I said, "I am wearing a disguise. I haven't handled a pitchfork for years, but I've served my apprenticeship. I'm Curt Curran."

For a long moment we stood in silence simply staring at one another, and again a strange feeling came over me, that I had known this woman before, that she was something very special, and I was going to know her very well again. Something passed between us. I cannot describe it and I have too rational a mind to believe in love at first sight. No, it wasn't that. Rather, I suppose, a feeling of respect, of admiration, that this was a remarkably able and independent woman.

I didn't know what was going on in her mind, but she shivered and shook her head as if coming back to the reality of the moment. She took the glove off her right hand and extended it. She said, "I'm Judy Bishop. I could use some help. I'm slow getting my hay crop in. I just lost a man who was working for me."

"Have you got another fork?" I asked.

"You'll find one leaning against the wall just inside the barn door," she said.

"I'll get it," I said.

Still, I didn't move for a moment, perhaps not wanting it to end. She was, as I said, a big woman, but I had never seen a woman more feminine or more perfectly proportioned. She had dark eyes, a lock of black hair showed against her forehead just under her hat brim, and her skin was as brown as a cowboy's. Her face held wrinkles from sun and wind, but certainly not from age. She was, I sense, about my age.

Suddenly she smiled. "Well, Mr. Curran, if you're going to help me, you'll have to go get the pitchfork."

I turned to my horse and mounted. "I was just thinking that you are a most unusual woman, Miss . . ."

"Mrs. Bishop," she said. "The 'Mrs.' doesn't mean much as far as the work is concerned. My husband died last year and I can't afford a full-time ranch hand, so I work the ranch myself if that's what you mean by being unusual."

"It is," I said. "My services are free for whatever they're worth."

I rode toward the barn, sensing that the man she had lost was Gordy Morgan. My assignment wasn't over by a long shot, but he had been here, and maybe Judy Bishop knew where he had gone.

I found the pitchfork exactly where Judy had said it would be and rode back to the wagon with it. I tied my horse behind the wagon, unlatched my gun belt and draped it over the horn, then I went to work pitching hay onto the load with Judy doing the spreading. It was soon topped out and she drove to the barn while I mounted and rode behind the wagon.

I climbed into the mow and Judy pitched the hay to me through a small door. I had to hustle to keep the hay out of the opening, and since there was a good deal of hay already in the mow, I had to move each forkful to the back. By the time the last of the load was off the wagon, I was puffing and huffing and realizing I was not in shape to be a hay hand.

When I got down, Judy said, "Put your horse in the corral. There's no sense of you working in that suit. You'll find some work clothes in the bunkhouse." She nodded toward a log cabin that was set between the house and the barn and slightly to the back.

"I'll go see if any of it fits me," I said as I wiped my face with a handkerchief. "It's hotter'n hades in that mow."

She laughed. "I know. I'll trade you jobs next time, unless you've had enough and want to quit."

I looked down at my hands where blisters were already starting to form. "No, I'm not ready to quit, but I would like a pair of gloves."

"You'll find some in the bunkhouse," she said, and climbed on the wagon and drove back into the field.

It took me a good part of an hour to unsaddle, let my horse into the corral, and find clothes that would fit me. I found a number of shirts and pants that were fairly new. I guessed they belonged to her husband. In any case they were all the same size, so I had no choice. The man who had worn them was bigger than I was, but that was better than if he had been smaller.

By the time I got back to the wagon, she had the load nearly finished. There was time for only one more load that morning. She said, "We'll knock off and eat dinner. You've probably worked up an appetite by now."

"I guess so," I said. "All I know is that I have a hollow place where my stomach ought to be."

We walked toward the house, Judy eyeing me as if something about me didn't quite add up. Finally she said, "I can't believe you were just riding around looking for a job."

"I wasn't," I said. "When I saw you loading that wagon by yourself, I figured you needed some help. I'm here because I'm a reporter for the *Rocky Mountain News.* I'd give you one of my cards, but I left them in my suit."

"Don't tell me you're writing a story about haying," she said tartly.

It was plain she didn't believe me and it was important to me that she did. I said, "No, a job pitching hay wasn't in my plans. I'm trying to get the truth about Gordy Morgan, and to do that I need to talk to him. I understand he's been working for you."

She shook her head. "I don't think I ever heard of Gordy Morgan. The man who was working for me was named John Smith. Does the law want this Gordy Morgan you're talking about?"

"No," I answered. "He killed some men on the other side of Trinidad and the father of one of the men he killed is hunting for him." We had almost reached the house. I stopped as I said, "I have reason to believe your John Smith is Gordy Morgan."

She shrugged her shoulders. "All I know is that he gave his name as John Smith and he was a good worker." She stopped and looked back at me. "But he was running from somebody. He'd been working here a month or more, then yesterday he left without giving any reason."

"You have any idea where he went?"

"No." She paused and frowned. "How did you hear he was working for me?"

"I heard it in Stonewall."

"Did Mack Olney, the hotel man, tell you?"

I shook my head. "I promised not to tell who told me."

"It must have been the boy Larry," she said. "He's not quite bright, you know. He has fantasies." She jerked her head at the back door. "Come on in. My daughter will have dinner ready."

I followed her into the kitchen. I wasn't convinced that Larry had had a fantasy about Gordy Morgan working here, but so far I didn't have any evidence that it was Gordy. I was going to stay here for a while and find out. I was just working on another of my hunches.

CHAPTER XVII

As soon as we stepped into the kitchen Judy introduced me to her daughter Cindy. The girl was about sixteen or seventeen, I judged, small and pretty and as graceful as a young doe. She was about as timid, I thought. She shook hands with me, a firm grip that impressed me, then she turned immediately and began putting food on the table.

Judy and I washed up at a sink near the back door. Judy took her hat off, ran a hand over her hair, and then pumped a pan of water. She was more unconcerned about her appearance than any other woman I had ever seen. The situation here simply amazed me, two women running a ranch by themselves, no neighbors, and the nearest town several miles away. Judy was a mature woman who had made her choice, but I wondered about Cindy, young and pretty and with no social life whatever.

The meal was good: ham, biscuits, honey, potatoes, carrots, coffee, and a slab of custard pie. We didn't talk. We simply ate, Judy with unabashed relish, Cindy picking at her food, and I guess I made a pig of myself because I had trouble filling the hole that was my stomach.

Judy had made no explanation of my presence when she introduced me, and Cindy hadn't asked. Now Judy said, "Mr. Curran is here to find out about a young man named Gordy Morgan. Mr. Curran is a reporter from the *Rocky Mountain News*."

Cindy seemed startled when she heard Gordy's name, but she only said, "Oh," as if it meant nothing to her.

"Your mother tells me you had a young man working here named John Smith," I said. "I think he is the Gordy Morgan I'm looking for. He would be interested in knowing that the law doesn't want him."

"His name is John Smith," she said, not looking at me.

"Do you know where he went when he left here?" I asked.

"No," she said.

She rose and went into another room and shut the door. Judy got up and, going to the stove, picked up the coffee pot and brought it to the table. She filled our cups and set the pot back on the stove. She sat down and looked at me, deeply troubled.

"I've got a problem I don't know how to handle," she said. "Cindy has been after me to sell and move into town, but I like it here and I'm going to stay. Cindy has never attended an school except a girls' boarding school in Trinidad. She's never been around boys. John Smith showed up and wanted a job. He had a good appearance that I liked, so I hired him, and Cindy fell in love with him."

"How did she take it when he left?" I asked.

"It hit her hard, but I think she knows where he went," Judy said. "As a matter of fact, I don't think he's gone very far. I don't know that for sure. Oh, and there's another thing. We know that a couple of men have been watching this place for a week. They came here once and wanted to search the house for a man they said was wanted by the law. They claimed to be deputies, but they didn't have stars or badges of any kind. When I insisted on seeing a warrant, they left."

"Did they see John Smith?"

"No, he stayed in the barn."

"Why did he leave?" I asked. "Was it right after the men were here?"

"No, that was several days ago," she said. "He was awfully uneasy after they were here, but it wasn't until we saw sunlight flashing on a glass on top of Sugar Loaf that he pulled out. I rode up there and found these same two men camped there. One of them was watching us through a pair of binoculars. I told him when I got back. He was gone within the hour."

"Was he about eighteen, redhaired, with a short red beard?" I asked, "And did he walk with a slight limp?"

She stared at me as if I had shocked her, then she nodded. She said, "That's just about perfect except that I would have guessed him a little older."

"He's Gordy Morgan, all right," I said. "If Cindy knows where he is, she ought to tell him to see me. I won't hurt him. All I want is a chance to talk to him. Besides, he should know the law isn't after him."

"If he killed four men," she said, "why isn't the law after him?"

I told her what had happened as quickly as I could, then said, "The only reason I'm here is because my boss has a good nose for news and he thought that Gordy was getting a crooked deal from the Trinidad *Tribune*, so he sent me down here to get the true story. I've got most of it, but I still need to talk to Gordy. The sheriff would like to know about the man he killed in the hotel room in Trinidad, but if he says it was self defense, Garcia will probably believe him.

"The strange part of the whole deal is that it's all tangled up with Garcia hating Pettit and Pettit hating Garcia and doing all he can to get him out of office. I suppose that if Garcia is beaten in the election this fall, the new sheriff will probably issue a warrant for Gordy's arrest, unless Pettit holds him off so he can finish Gordy himself."

"Sounds like a lot of probablys to me," Judy said. "Gordy is better off to stay a free man."

"He'll stay a free man as far as I'm concerned," I said. "What he ought to know is that these men who are looking for him are private detectives. If they find him, they'll hold him for Pettit."

"And Pettit will kill him," she said as she rose. "Let's go to work."

We didn't talk much that afternoon, but I did learn that Judy and her husband had come here as a young married couple, had bought the place when there was nothing here but a small, one-room cabin. They had slowly built up the ranch, developed a small herd of whitefaces, and raised a few good horses.

"A cattle buyer comes to Stonewall every fall," she said, "and we always have a few steers to sell. Mack Olney in the hotel buys horses each fall and we always had two or three good young saddle horses to sell that brought a premium price. That's all the income we have. Usually we keep the heifers. We have chickens and a sow. We butcher one steer a year, or a barren heifer. We have a big garden. We can have venison or an elk when we want them. There are trout in the creek and some big ones in the pond, so we fare pretty well."

We were riding back to the field when she said this. When we reached the first shock, she said, "It's been a good life for me, Mr. Curran. I hope I can keep it."

"I'm going to be here a while," I said. "I'd like to call you Judy and have you call me Curt."

"Good," she said, "but I can't figure you staying here."

"It's the only lead I've got to where Gordy is," I said. "I don't see any sense in going back to Trinidad, and I sure as hell can't go home yet until I've used up every chance I've got to find Gordy. My boss never likes an unfinished story. Gordy will turn up here. I've got a hunch."

She stood looking down at me and I looked up at her, my pitchfork rammed into the shock of hay. We stood motionless for a time, and again I sensed that strange feeling between us. I cannot analyze it or name it, but it was a good feeling, and I blurted, "Besides, I like it here."

"I hoped you would," she said, and laughed. "At least until we get the hay in."

When we knocked off that evening, she said, "Why don't you take a swim? I usually do after a day's work. You'll find a gravel bottom on this side of the pond. I guess the creek used to go through there. Everywhere else the pond has a muddy bottom." She paused and smiled, adding, "You don't need to worry about anyone spying on you."

I wanted to ask her to come and go swimming with me, but that would have been absurd, knowing her only a few hours. I was afraid she would have been offended. Still, she might have done it. She'd told me she was more comfortable with men than women, that woman talk drove her crazy. She had never, she said, missed the company of women, and she had never gone to the women's club meetings in Stonewall. She was like no other woman I had ever met, with none of the devious woman wiles that more than once had turned me away from girls I might have wanted to marry.

As soon as the horses were taken care of, I took her suggestion. I was tired and sweaty, and I knew my muscles would be so sore the next day I probably would regret my decision to stay. I found the gravel bottom she had mentioned. I took off my clothes and waded into the pond until the water was up to my waist and then started to swim. The water was warm and relaxing, and I had never appreciated a swim more in my life than I did that one.

I had gone across the pond twice and returned when I heard Judy yelling at me. I saw her running toward me carrying a pitchfork and motioning wildly to the east. I was irritated because I barely had time to pull my drawers on before she reached me. I wondered what she was doing with the pitchfork, but I didn't ask.

She was panting when she got to me and still making wild gestures toward the east. She said, "We have trouble, Curt."

I pulled on my shirt and started buttoning it as I stepped away from the willows that blocked my view to the east. I saw two men riding toward us. One was the Jerry Hahn I had seen in Stonewall who claimed he was selling encyclopedias. I didn't recognize the other man, but by the time I had finished pulling on my pants and buckling my belt, they were close enough for me to recognize the second man as Slim Akins, a Denver bunco artist who had spent more time in jail than out. He had been associated with Soapy Smith and Hank De Bussy in the old days, so there wasn't much doubt about why he was here now. I stood staring at them and mentally cursing myself for leaving my gun in the bunkhouse.

The men rode up to us and dismounted. I said, "Hahn, I'm still not in the market for an encyclopedia."

He looked at me as if he thought I was an idiot, then turned to Judy. "We're going to search your house, Mrs. Bishop, and don't get smart like telling us to get a warrant. Somebody is going to get hurt if you do." He pulled a gun out from under his coat. "This is all the warrant we need."

"You tried this once before, didn't you?" I asked, "and then you had to go back to Trinidad to talk to your boss. Since you were coming back here anyhow, he put you on my tail. That right?"

"That's about it," he said. "Now we think Gordy Morgan was here a few days ago. If he's in the house now, we aim to get him."

"I'd about as soon let a rabid skunk into my house as you," Judy said, "but it wouldn't do you any good if you did search the place. He's gone and I don't know where he went."

"You're lying," Hahn said. "We'll see for ourselves. You go first, Mrs. Bishop, so Morgan won't start shooting at us. We'll be right behind you."

"You've changed games, haven't you, Akins?" I asked. "The last I saw of you, you were being charged with selling gold bricks that didn't have much gold in them."

He shrugged and grinned. "You go where the money is, Curran. Selling gold bricks ain't a real profitable business any more."

"Come on, come on," Hahn said, turning his gun so that he covered me. "I'm not a patient man, Mrs. Bishop. Now you get moving or your new hay hand will be picking lead out of his brisket."

I didn't know whether Akins had a gun or not, but from his history, I judged he was not a violent man. I guessed that Hahn was, so it struck me that the odds would be on Judy's side if it came to her tangling with Akins. My job was to jump Hahn, but it would have been suicide if I tackled him when his gun was on me. I held back, waiting for Judy to make a move, and she did the only thing she could have done.

"You don't give me much choice," she said.

She took a step toward Akins. I don't know what he thought she was up to, or whether he even thought about it, but he turned to move around Hahn. I supposed he aimed to lead the horses to the house, but before he reached them, Judy suddenly lifted her pitchfork and jabbed him in the ass. He jumped about three feet and let out a yelp you could have heard a mile away.

Hahn expected me to make the trouble if there was any, so he had kept his eyes on me. When he heard Akin's howl of pain, he turned to see what the yelling was all about. I was near enough to close the distance between us before he could swing back. He fired one shot that went wild, and then I hit his right wrist with a downward slice of my left hand that was hard enough to knock the gun loose.

I came in fast and bowled him over. He fell on his back and I jumped on him, my knees driving his breath out of him. For an instant he was helpless. I rolled him over on his belly and dragged him across the gravel to the edge of the pond. I jammed his head into the water and held it there while he kicked and squirmed and fought, but I was bigger than he was and I kept his nose and mouth in the water. I was mad enough to drown him and I think I would have if Judy hadn't yelled, "Don't drown him, Curt. Don't drown him."

Her words finally got through to me and I yanked Hahn out of the water and turned him on his back. He got part way up and finally managed to get on his hands and knees, his head down, the water running out of his mouth and nose as he coughed and hacked and sputtered.

I pulled him to his feet as I said, "Get on your horse. Get out of here and don't come back. Tell De Bussy that Gordy Morgan is gone and I don't know where he is."

"You, too," Judy said to Akins. "Get on your horse and don't stay camped on Sugar Loaf. That's my range and I'm not standing for any trespassing."

They mounted, Hahn still choking and fighting for breath, and Akins whimpering like a stepped-on pup. We stood watching them ride away. I said, "Did you have that in mind when you brought the pitchfork?"

"No," she answered. "I didn't have a gun in the barn, and I couldn't see any other weapon." She laughed, and I knew from the sound that she was almost hysterical. “Anyhow, it worked.”

I nodded, still watching them, but I was sure of one thing. We hadn’t seen the last of them.

CHAPTER XVIII

I had trouble sleeping that night, partly because I discovered more sore spots than I knew I had muscles, but mostly because I was uneasy. I had no idea what orders De Bussy had given his men, but I was convinced that they would make some kind of retaliatory move. I had told Judy to bar both the front and back doors, something which she usually did not do. Still, I knew it wasn’t enough because a man can always get into a house if he’s determined to search the house for Gordy.

Finally I got up, pulled on my pants and boots, and buckled my gun belt around me. The night was warm, with a full moon. I walked around the house, then around all of the buildings, and I saw nothing out of the way. Just as I was about to go back to the bunkhouse, I froze. Someone was coming across the pasture.

I stepped into the shadow of the woodshed which was just back of the kitchen door and waited, my hand on the butt of my gun. I couldn’t tell who it was until she was close, then I saw it was Cindy. I stayed where I was until she was opposite me, then I said, "You've been to see Gordy?"

She cried out in surprise and made a dash for the back porch, but I had anticipated that and caught her before she reached the door. I said, "You're going to talk to me, so don't make a fight out of it."

She didn't. She trembled as she looked up at me, then she said, "Keep your voice down. I don't want to wake ma."

"All right," I said. "Where is he?"

"He's hiding back in the timber," she said, "but he comes to the edge of the pasture every night. I take grub to him. I told him about you wanting to see him, but he said he doesn't have anything to say to you."

"Then he's an idiot," I said. "When and if I get all of his story, I'll be able to undo some of the damage the Trinidad *Tribune* has done to his reputation. Can't he figure out that in the long run it will be public opinion that frees him or jails him?"

"He's scared, Mr. Curran," she said. "He said up until the night he left Lark, he had never been afraid of anything, but now the whole world is after him and he doesn't know where to go or what to do. I asked him to stay and see what you can do for him, but I think he's going to run again. If he does, I'm going with him."

I thought of Cissy back in Lark and how she had

said she would go with Gordy, and he had said she would slow him down. Now I wondered how he felt about Cindy going with him. I never know how much a man should interfere in another person's life, but in general I have found that the safest and most reasonable thing for everyone is to stay out completely. My interest was my story. Beyond that, what Cindy did was her business.

"I'll go with you tomorrow night," I said. "I'll talk to him."

"No," she said. "He'll kill you if you do, so don't try it. He thinks everybody is against him, including you and the Trinidad sheriff. He told me he had never killed anyone he didn't have to, but he says after killing four men, he'll kill anyone who tries to take him."

I wondered again as I had so many times just what kind of man Gordy Morgan was. Still, I could understand what had happened to him, wounded and on the run with a powerful man such as Saul Pettit after him wanting to kill him, and without friends after he had left Pete Grimes. Apparently he thought they wanted him, too. He had probably thought he had a safe refuge here until De Bussy's men had showed up, and now he was, or thought he was, being forced to flee from here.

Finally I said, "All right, Cindy, I won't try to talk to him unless he's willing to talk to me, but keep trying to persuade him to see me. I can help him. I think he'll have to surrender himself sooner or later. If he doesn't, Pettit will kill him eventually. I don't think he'll ever give up. Right now the sheriff feels friendly toward him and I think he would believe him, but that may change."

"I'll try," she whispered, "but I don't think he'll ever give himself up. He says he's so tired of running that he'd rather die than keep on the way he's been living."

"Be sure to bar the door when you go in," I said, and released my grip on her arm.

After I went back to bed, I asked myself if I should tell Judy what I had learned. It would be crazy for Cindy to run off with Gordy when he left, but I had a hunch she was that crazy. If she did, Judy would be hard hit. I didn't think there was any way that Judy could make Cindy stay. After all, the girl was eighteen years old. In the end I decided it was between Judy and Cindy, and it would be a mistake for me to interfere.

Every night I expected some kind of attack, but the days passed and it didn't come. I spoke to Cindy every night when she returned from seeing Gordy, but it was always the same. He refused to talk to me. He didn't even believe me when I sent word that the law didn't want him.

By the end of the week my muscles had hardened up so that most of the soreness was gone. We finished the hay, stacking all that was left after the mow was filled. Judy expected me to leave then, but I didn't want to go. As long as Gordy was around, I had an excuse to stay.

I asked Judy if there was any other work to do. She looked at me as if I didn't have good sense. She said, "Curt, there never was a day when there wasn't work to be done around here. I don't even have the winter's wood cut."

So that was the next job. On the following morning we lifted the hayrack off the running gear and set the wood rack in its place. We set out for a patch of windfall pines on the slope of one of the foothills to the west of the house. It was September now, and the first snow of the fall had iced the Sangre de Cristo peaks with a white frosting. The air definitely had the feel of fall, and Judy worried that we wouldn't get enough wood in before the heavy snow came.

It happened that night after I had begun to think that nothing was going to happen. I had seen Cindy after she got home from her visit with Gordy and had gone to bed. I had just dropped off to sleep when a rifle shot woke me. By sheer instinct I rolled out of bed as glass tinkled to the floor.

Another rifle opened up farther to the east as I crawled across the room to my Winchester that leaned against the wall near the foot of the bunk. Apparently the first man was firing at the house. The moon was far from full, so they didn't have much light to shoot by. They must, I thought, be reasonably close, perhaps at the barn or the corral.

I reached my Winchester, then crawled to the door and opened it a crack. The man who had fired at the bunkhouse was still shooting, but now he was aiming at the house. From the flash of the rifle fire, I judged he was crouched at the corner of the corral, so I levered a shell into the chamber and squeezed the trigger. I heard a yelp, but I wasn't sure it was a sound of pain. Maybe I had come close enough to scare him.

I fired two more times, then pulled back from the door. It was a good thing I did because his next shot splintered the door casing inches from where I had been crouched a few seconds earlier and slapped into the log wall behind me. I moved to the window, knocked out more of the glass, and fired two more times from there, then I pulled back.

Somebody started firing from the house. It had to be Judy. I didn't think Cindy had the stomach for it. I wasn't sure where the second man was located, but I guessed it was somewhere along the edge of the pond.

The firing stopped as suddenly as it had begun. I stayed in the bunkhouse quite a while, not sure whether the men had left or were waiting for us to show ourselves. I opened the door and slipped outside, putting my back against the wall, then waited some more. I thought I heard horses off to the east, but I wasn't sure. I had to know if Judy was all right, so I ran to the house, keeping low and hoping there wasn't enough light for them to see me if they were still out there.

I paused at the corner of the house and called, "Judy, let me in."

I eased along the front wall of the house and called again, "It's me, Judy."

The door banged open and I charged through it and bumped into Judy who had laid her rifle down. I put a hand out to her in the darkness, but she wasn't content with a hand. She threw her arms around me and hugged me, crying out, "Are you all right, Curt?"

"I'm fine," I said. "How about you?"

"I'm still in one piece," she said, and reluctantly, I thought, released me.

"Cindy?" I asked.

"I'm all right," she said from somewhere in the back of the room.

Judy had closed the door and barred it, then struck a match and lit a lamp. Cindy was standing in the kitchen doorway, trembling and tearful, but Judy wasn't trembling and she sure wasn't crying. She was just plain mad. She motioned to the bullet-splintered windows.

"Look what they did," she said. "Look at that. And why? What did they think they were accomplishing?"

"Scaring us," I said. "I think they're convinced

that you're hiding Gordy and if they do this a few times, you'll give him up."

"A few times," she said, her voice crackling with emotion. "There won't be a few times. We're going to run the bastards off Sugar Loaf in the morning."

CHAPTER XIX

We ate breakfast by lamplight, Cindy nervous and tired, her hair down her back in an unruly, black mass. Judy was her old self, exuberant and excited as if she actually looked forward to the day's mission, but Cindy was worried. I didn't ask her what was wrong, thinking she wouldn't say anything in front of her mother.

Sugar Loaf was a bald mountain two miles or so east of the BB buildings. Judy had pointed it out to me the first morning I was here and we had watched it several times. When the sun was right, we could nearly always glimpse a flash of light on a pair of glasses, so we knew we were being spied on just as they had spied on the ranch before Gordy left.

Now, as we saddled up and started out, I began to wish I had made a more serious effort to contact Gordy instead of waiting hopefully for him to send word that he was willing to talk to me. I had one of my hunches that the violence last night was all it would take to start him running again. I had just about decided that if he did, I'd let him go, that I'd chased him long enough and I had all the story I was going to get.

Judy did not take a direct route to the top of Sugar Loaf, but circled to the north, following a game trail that led through the quakies. We were in the open for a time before we reached a belt of pines that lay just below the bald peak of the mountain. I judged this was the reason she had started so early, that if we had made the trip in full daylight, they could have seen us from their camp site.

The first arc of the sun was beginning to show above the horizon when we reined up. She said, "Bring your rifle, Curt. We'll leave the horses here."

We dismounted, tied our mounts, and eased forward through the fringe of trees until we reached the edge of the rounded bald top of Sugar Loaf. A tent was directly ahead of us. A man was bending over a fire in front of it fussing over a coffee pot. Hahn, I judged from his size. He had his back to us so I couldn't see his face.

"We'll pour it to them," Judy said with satisfaction. "We'll let 'em see how it feels to be on the other end of a shooting."

"I'm not here to do any killing," I said, "If you're figuring on . . ."

"I'm not," she said, "unless we scare 'em to

death. We'll tell 'em to slope out of here but if they ever come back, we *will* kill 'em."

We lay down behind the trunk of a windfall pine and started shooting. My first bullet took the coffee pot out from under Hahn's nose and he sprawled straight back and fell flat. After that we laced our bullets through the tent. Akins came stumbling out with nothing on but his drawers, his hands in the air, yelling, "Don't shoot. Don't shoot." Hahn bounced to his feet, his hands above his head.

"I guess we're wasting our lead," Judy said as if she was sorry the show was over. "We'll go up there and palaver."

We walked up the slope, our Winchesters on the ready. Neither man said a word, but Hahn was mad and Akins was scared; there wasn't any fight left in either one. We didn't say anything until we were within ten feet of them, then Judy motioned to Akins as she said, "Get dressed. If you come out of that tent with a gun in your hand, your partner will be so full of lead you won't recognize him."

Akins disappeared inside. Hahn asked, "You aiming to beef us?"

"After last night you couldn't blame us if we did," Judy answered. "I don't like getting my house shot up. No, I'm not going to kill you. I want you to go back to whoever hired you and tell him I'm not hiding Gordy Morgan, I don't know where he is, and I don't want to know. What's more, I will kill you or anyone else who comes around here looking for him. Now get on your horses and vamoose."

They didn't wait for a second invitation. Their horses were staked out downslope from us. We pulled the tent down and threw it and their blankets on the fire. Judy found a sack and partly filled it with ham, bacon, flour, and other groceries that had been inside the tent. By that time both men had saddled their horses and had mounted. They headed toward the fringe of timber below us to the south. Judy picked up her rifle and fired a couple of shots over their heads to hurry them along.

"Think they'll stay away now?" she asked.

"Akins will," I said. "I'm not sure about Hahn. He's a killer and this is going to be a burr under his saddle, but Hank De Bussy is smart enough. He may decide he's played this hand for all it's worth."

We walked down the slope to our horses, mounted, and took the direct trail that led to the BB buildings. I said, "Did you ever think that Cindy might run off with Gordy when he leaves?"

Judy shook her head. "Cindy and I have our differences, but she wouldn't run away."

I let it go at that, thinking that nothing I could say would convince Judy that Cindy would run off with Gordy, and that she couldn't do anything about it at this point anyhow.

Before we reached the house, I said, "I'm going to Stonewall. Didn't you tell me that Mack Olney was a deputy?"

She nodded. "He doesn't work very hard at it, but he's a good friend of the sheriff and gets word to him if anything is wrong out here. Usually Garcia shows up right away and handles the trouble if there is any."

"I'm going to order new windows," I said, "and I'm going to tell Olney to have Garcia come out and search your buildings. When he doesn't find Gordy, maybe that will convince De Bussy that Gordy isn't here."

I was afraid she wouldn't let Garcia on her property and that would give me a problem, but she wasn't that bullheaded. She nodded and said, "I'm sick and tired of the whole business. If you think that would stop it, we'll give Garcia an invitation. Oh, and pick up the mail when you're there."

I nodded and turned south, and a few minutes later struck the road that led to Stonewall. I found Mack Olney behind the desk in the hotel. I hadn't paid much attention to him before when I was here except to notice the obvious, that he was an elderly, slender man who was efficient at his job, but now I gave him a second look. Still, I didn't see any more than I had the first time. I had met men before who seemed very ordinary, but were far more than that when I had time and opportunity to know them. I suspected that was true with Mack Olney. He was, according to Judy, Mr. Everything around Stonewall.

He recognized me immediately even though I was wearing work clothes and I'd had my suit on when I'd been here before. He asked, "Did you find the young man you were looking for?"

"No," I said. "He had been working for Mrs. Bishop, but quit just before I got there. I'm working for her now."

"Good," he said. "She needs a man. She has ever since her husband died, but she and Cindy have managed."

"You lied to me," I said. "You knew he had been through here."

He smiled. "Why yes, I did, didn't I? I lie only for friends, and Judy Bishop is a very good friend and has been for years. You see, she asked me to say I hadn't seen him. She knew he was running from somebody, but she didn't know why or who."

"Now that's a funny thing," I said. "He might have been running from the law, and I understand you're a deputy."

"I thought about that," he admitted, "but I trust Judy's judgment. I figured he wasn't a man who was wanted by the law if he was a man she trusted. Anyhow, the sheriff always gets word to me to watch for anyone who's wanted for a crime in this county." He paused, then added, "And I'm not what you call an active deputy. I haven't made an arrest for more than a year."

"But you do keep in touch with Garcia?"

"You bet I do." He nodded. "If anything is really wrong out here, I call Carlos, and he comes out and makes the arrest if one is necessary."

"You remember the man who calls himself Jerry Hahn?"

Olney nodded again. "Of course. He was here the night you stayed with us. As a matter of fact, I've wondered about him. He's been in and out of Stonewall several times."

"He works for a Denver detective agency," I said. "He's with another Denver man named Slim Akins who has been a notorious con man for years. They thought Mrs. Bishop was hiding Gordy Morgan, the young man you know as John Smith."

"Gordy Morgan," he mused. "Killed three men, I believe. A vicious Billy the Kid type according to the *Tribune*."

"It's a lie," I said. "The sheriff says all the killings were justified homicides, but that's not why I'm here. Hahn and Akins have been watching Mrs. Bishop's place for some time. They rode up one evening and Hahn threw a gun on me and said they were going to search the place for Gordy, but Mrs. Bishop wouldn't allow it. We managed to turn the tables on them and ran them off, but last night they shot the place up and knocked out some of our windows."

"You want them arrested?"

"No," I said. "We chased them off Sugar Loaf this morning where they were camped and I think they'll go to town, but I don't think they believed us when we said Gordy wasn't there. I want you to ask Garcia to come out and search the place himself. He would have a legal right to do it and Judy will let him make the search. She never would let Hahn or his boss do it. Maybe Hahn's boss will believe the sheriff and that'll get them off our backs."

"Sure, I'll call him today," Olney promised, "but why would the sheriff ride all the way out here if Morgan isn't wanted by the law?"

"There was a fourth killing in Trinidad which hasn't been explained to Garcia," I said. "He wants to ask Gordy some questions about it."

I told him to order new windows and he said they would be there on the next day's stage. I picked up Judy's mail and left. It was after noon when I got back. I found Judy sitting at the kitchen table as if she were frozen. I had never seen a human being as distraught and broken as she was.

She stared at me as if I were a stranger. She said, "Cindy's gone. She ran off with Gordy."

CHAPTER XX

We didn't have any dinner that day, but I wasn't any hungrier than Judy was. I spent the afternoon in the bunkhouse bringing my news story up to date. I hadn't sent anything to the Great Man for more than a week, so he'd be after my scalp if I didn't get something to him. I hated to leave loose ends dangling, but that was the way it was going to be this time. Gordy Morgan was gone.

I didn't know if Judy felt like cooking any more than she had at noon, but when I finished, I went into the kitchen to find out. I was hungry, and if she wasn't going to cook, I was. I had no reason to worry. She had supper almost ready to go on the table.

"I'm glad you came in," she said. "I was just about to ring the dinner bell." She carried a dish of potatoes to the table. "I'm out of practice, so this meal may not be fit to eat. Cindy has done the cooking for a long time. When my husband was alive, I was outside with him more than I was in the house. I like to work outside and Cindy liked to do housework, so it was a natural division of labor." She brought a dish of beans to the table and wiped her forehead. "But it's going to be different now."

She motioned for me to sit down, poured the

coffee, then took a chair opposite me. She said, "You knew, didn't you?"

"Not for sure," I answered. "She told me she was thinking of going with him, but I didn't know how serious she was."

"She was serious enough," Judy said glumly. "Now I'm alone. I've never been more alone in my life."

"I'm here," I said.

She looked up from her plate, startled. "But you won't be here much longer."

"Would you like it if I was?" I found myself leaning forward as I waited for her answer, and when it didn't come for a moment I asked, "I mean, here to stay?"

She still didn't answer for a time, her gaze riveted on her plate, then she looked up, and I was surprised to see tears in her eyes. "This is crazy talk, Curt. Don't tease me. I don't feel like it tonight. Eat your supper. I've got something to show you when you're done."

I let it go at that. This wasn't the time to tell her how I felt. She was right. It was crazy talk, crazy to even think of being in love with a woman I had known only a little more than a week. But I knew I was.

As soon as I was done eating, she rose and went into her bedroom. She returned a moment later with a notebook, the kind a high school student would use for class notes. She said, "This is

Gordy's diary. I guess he left in such a hurry he forgot it. He told me he had kept a diary ever since he'd been a small boy, that he'd filled several notebooks, but he'd left them at home. He didn't really tell me why he kept it except that it helped him remember things that he would otherwise forget."

As I opened it, I remembered that Jonathan Aldridge had told me about his diary. I had never known anyone who kept a diary, and it seemed strange that a boy like Gordy would do it, but Gordy was a strange boy. The more I learned about him, the less I felt I knew him.

He had started this book in May about the time school was out. Apparently he had written the first two pages before graduation while he was still home; then, after getting to Pete Grimes' place, he had written more. He wrote well, I thought, but not as well as Jonathan Aldridge had indicated. I was familiar with the first part of the narrative which jibed with what I had learned when I had been in Lark, then I came to the night Bud Pettit was killed and I couldn't believe what I was reading:

> "I had been in love with Cissy as long as I can remember. I thought she loved me, although I know she had a reputation of being a flirt. I knew she had dates with Bud, but she told me she loved me, that

she was just stringing Bud along and for me not to worry. Ed told me I was crazy to believe her, but I did anyhow.

"If I'd had good sense, I would have taken Zach Wheeler's advice and left the country after we finished burying Ed. I dug up pa's gold that was under the hearth, about $600, enough to get me far enough away until I could get a job and make my living and not worry about the law or Pettit catching up with me. Someday I would go back and settle with Pettit for what he had done to me and my family. I'm convinced he murdered pa, but I have no proof. I do know what happened to Ed and what would happen to me if Pettit caught me after I had shot his two hands.

"But no, I wasn't endowed with good sense because I had to see Cissy before I left and I even had the wild idea she would go away with me, so I waited until I figured everybody was asleep, then I rode to the Edwards house and tapped on Cissy's window until she woke up and lit a lamp.

"She opened the window and climbed through it. She kissed me and acted as if she was glad to see me, but she kept me in the lamplight. I didn't even realize she was doing it, but now I know she was and

I know why. She was fixing it so Bud could kill me. When I asked her to go with me, she laughed and said why should she go with me and starve to death when she could marry a rich man's son.

"I heard Bud yell at her to get away from me. I whirled around and drew my gun, but before I could pull the trigger, I saw Bud standing in front of me, I saw the flash of gunpowder, and I felt his bullet hit me in the left arm. It turned me partly around but I got off my shot. I saw him fall. I heard Cissy scream that I had killed him, then I knelt down beside him and I saw I really had killed him. Now that I had killed his son, I knew that Saul Pettit would never give up on me until I was dead. I ran to my horse and got out of there as fast as I could. I heard Cissy scream for a long time."

I sat there staring at the diary for five minutes before I turned a page. This just didn't jibe at all with what Cissy Edwards had told me. The question was which one was lying. Cissy had no reason to lie. Gordy had no reason to lie in his diary. But then maybe Cissy did have a reason. Now that Bud was dead, she couldn't marry him. Gordy had always been more popular with the Lark people. Perhaps she thought that what she told me would be in the newspaper and her neighbors would read it, but if her neighbors ever heard that she had lured Gordy into a trap so Bud could kill him, she would be a pariah.

On the other hand, considering Gordy's side, I could see less reason for him to lie in his diary. He had no reason to expect anyone else to read it. Or maybe he wasn't lying, but had not given Cissy the right motives.

She might not even have thought about keeping him in the pool of lamplight under her window. I remembered that someone had told me there was a full moon that night, so the lamplight hadn't been that important. It was very possible that she had not even known Bud was anywhere around there and that Gordy had jumped to the conclusion she knew and so had trapped him.

I shook my head in despair because there was no way to know the truth and I had a strong feeling I never would. I started reading again:

> "My arm was hurting like hell and I knew I had to find a place to hide. I thought Pete Grimes would help me. He had been a good friend of pa's and had always been good to Ed and me, and I knew he had no reason to love the Pettits, so I headed for the mesa. I got Pete out of bed and told him what had happened. He looked at my arm and said I'd better hole

up with him for a couple of weeks. He poured whiskey over the wound and tied a rag around it. He said it was a flesh wound and that the bone hadn't been touched, so I'd make it without a doctor.

"I stayed with Pete for two weeks and I think he was glad to have my company. He lived up there on the mesa by himself, so he was pretty much a hermit. The first day or so I didn't do much but lay on his bunk, but after that I got to feeling better, and we'd talk for hours at a time.

"Pettit's men came looking for me as I knew they would. Pete nailed some sacks over his window so nobody could look in and he kept the door barred. He said for me to bar it when he was out. He always knocked twice, paused, and knocked again when he wanted in. That way I wouldn't open the door to any of Pettit's crew.

"Pete's cabin had been used in the early days for a hide-out for outlaws. When he first moved in, he discovered that there was a trap door in the floor. When he lifted it, he found a small hole under it that was big enough for a man to hide in. He covered the trap door with a rag rug. Several times when Pettit's men were close, he had me hide in the hole. Usually they just took his word that he hadn't seen me. He was taking a big chance because if they had found me, they would have killed him."

This part jibed with what Pete had told me, and it explained how he had hid Gordy. The diary told how Gordy had come on into Trinidad to buy grub and a newspaper so he could see what was being said about him, but he never got the newspaper because he had his trouble with De Bussy's man. Of course he didn't know anything about De Bussy or that Pettit had hired a detective agency to find him.

The way Gordy told it, the man must have recognized him on the street or in the lobby from the description he had. He was waiting for him in his room, threw a gun on him, and said he was taking him to Lark. Gordy knew what would happen to him when he got to Lark, but he pretended to go along. He had a derringer in his pocket, so he faked getting his feet tangled up before he got to the door.

He had his hands in his pockets after taking off his gun belt. When he stumbled, he managed to lurch against his captor and knock him off stride. That gave him a chance to get the derringer out of his pocket and shoot the detective while the man was still trying to regain his balance. Since he'd killed four men, he figured he had no chance with the law, so he grabbed up his gun belt and dropped out of the window to the roof below him, got his horse, and rode out of town.

He didn't make it clear as to why he went up the Picketwire except that it took him off the usual avenues of travel and he guessed correctly that everyone would think he was headed for Mexico. He stayed one night at Stonewall. He had been careful about riding only at night after he left Trinidad, so he was foolish to come into the open and stay at the Stonewall Hotel. Again he didn't explain why he stayed there except to say he was hungry. If he hadn't eaten since he'd left Trinidad, he was hungry by the time he reached Stonewall.

He told about talking to Mack Olney and asking if there was any work around there and Olney suggested he try the BB which he did. He wrote in detail about irrigating and haying and helping with the chores, and about falling in love with Cindy. He had expected to stay here, but he admitted he was scared after the two men came to the house asking for him. That was the last thing he had written. When he and Judy realized the ranch was being watched, he must have decided it was time to hide.

I closed the diary and sat there thinking about it. The only place that I questioned was his talk with Cissy and his shooting Bud. The rest of it had the ring of truth in it, but by the time I got to the end, I began to have the feeling that Gordy was close to panic and not making sense in some of his decisions. Staying overnight at Stonewall was one. Even working so long for Judy was another. If he had gone on, he'd have been hundreds of miles away by now and the chances were good that De Bussy would never have picked up his trail again.

The thought occurred to me that maybe he was so tired of running that he really wanted to be caught, but hadn't realized it consciously. He was hiding out, but still he kept a daily contact with Cindy, and only after De Bussy's men had shot the place up, had he decided to run again and had taken Cindy with him. That was a mistake, too, because he would have gone faster without her and he would have been less conspicuous.

I looked up to see Judy watching me intently. She asked, "What do you think?"

"I don't know," I said. "Most of it sounds right. Have you read it?"

She nodded. "But not until today after Cindy left. I was going to ask about the other girl. I wondered if he fell in love with Cindy because they were about the same age and their names were a lot alike and maybe Cindy reminded him of her."

"It could be that way," I said. "I think he's about to do something crazy. He's had a lot of pressure on him after losing his father and his brother."

"Crazy?" She was startled. "But Cindy's with him."

I knew at once I shouldn't have said it. I didn't want to worry her, so I shrugged as if it wasn't important and said, "I don't think it will hurt Cindy. It's more likely he'll do something foolish like giving himself up just to get it over with."

"I wish I'd read the diary when I first found it," she said, "but I didn't because I thought it was private. After Cindy left with him, I didn't care. If I had read it, and I'd told Cindy about the other girl, she might not have gone with him."

"Don't blame yourself," I said. "Who knows what a girl in love will do?" I rose and yawned. "I'm going to bed. This has been quite a day."

"Curt . . ." She stopped, and then said slowly, "I don't like being alone in the house. Would you mind sleeping in Cindy's bed?"

"Of course not," I said.

For a moment I looked down at her, wondering if she really meant her bed but was too timid to say so or thought I might think she was too forward. I didn't see anything about her to indicate that. Later perhaps, I thought. But she needed more time.

CHAPTER XXI

I drove into Stonewall late the following afternoon to get the windows I had ordered and to mail what I thought would be the end of the Gordy Morgan story, at least as far as I was concerned. I had added very little after reading Gordy's diary. I couldn't relate the part in which he described the shooting with Bud Pettit. I would have if I had known it was true, but if it wasn't, I would be doing grave injury to Cissy Edwards.

I couldn't tell, either, now Pete Grimes had hidden Gordy when the Pettit men were searching for him. It would have given away Pete's secret of the trap door and brought Pettit's wrath down on his head. I did add how Gordy had shot the detective in the hotel room and escaped by jumping to the roof below him.

When I reached Stonewall, I mailed my envelope to the *Rocky Mountain News* and picked up the windows, then I asked Olney if he had been able to contact the sheriff. Olney nodded. "We'll be out there early Saturday morning. He wants me to go with him."

"Judy won't object to that," I said. "I guess Garcia knows Judy by reputation anyway."

"He does indeed," Olney said dryly.

Sure enough, we saw three men leave the timber south of the hay field Saturday morning soon after breakfast and ride toward the house. Garcia must have ridden to Stonewall on Friday and stayed the night in the hotel.

We watched them approach the house, Judy asking who the third man was. I didn't answer for a time because they were too far away to see their faces, but it didn't take me long to recognize Hank De Bussy. Long before I could see their faces clearly, I recognized the man's squat shape.

"It's De Bussy," I said. "He's the man who has the detective agency that hired the men who shot up your house."

She swore and took her Winchester down from the antler rack near the door. It was the first time I had heard her swear since I'd come here. She said, "He's not getting off his horse."

A few minutes later the three men reined up in front of the house. They touched the brims of their hats to Judy and all said, "Good morning." Then Olney started to say, "Judy, I guess you know the . . ."

"Yes, I know the sheriff." Judy was standing just outside her front door, her cocked rifle in her hands. "I also know who the bastard is that's sitting beside you, Mack. I don't know why you brought him, but I'll tell you one thing. If he so much as bats an eye or acts as if he's getting off his horse, I'll kill him. We haven't replaced the windows yet, Sheriff. I wanted you to see what his hired gun hands did."

Garcia looked at the bullet-shattered windows. "I see what somebody did, all right."

"Now you and Mack get down off your horses and search the place," Judy said. "Look into every closet in the house and under the rugs and into my chamber pot that's under my bed if you think it's big enough to hide Gordy Morgan. Look in all of my buildings. Curt, you go along with them. Then all three of you get to hell off my land."

Garcia and Olney stepped down. I almost laughed when I looked at Hank De Bussy's face. He was a very tough man, but right then he was also a very scared man. Garcia and Olney went into the house. I followed and watched them search every room. Then we left the house and tried the root cellar, the woodshed, the privy, the tool shed, the barn, and finally the bunkhouse.

"It was a waste of time," Olney said. "I knew it would be because Judy wouldn't lie to protect young Morgan, not to you."

"I figured it was," Garcia said, "but maybe this will get De Bussy off her back. It's a wonder somebody hasn't been killed."

"There will be," I said, "if he keeps harassing her. She's had all she's going to take."

"I don't blame her," Olney said. "Oh, where's Cindy? I expected to find her in the kitchen."

"She ran off with Gordy," I said.

"The hell she did." Olney stared at me as if he didn't believe it, then he shook his head sadly. "That's the last thing I thought that girl would do."

"That's what Judy thought," I said. "There's one more thing, Sheriff. Gordy is a diary keeper. I heard about his diary when I was in Lark. I guess he left all of the early part at home, but Judy found what he had written from the time of his graduation to when he left here. It doesn't tell us anything we didn't know except about the killing in the hotel room in Trinidad. He said the man was waiting for him in his room and threw a gun on him. He told Gordy he was taking him back to Lark. Gordy had a derringer in his pocket and managed to use it to kill the other man, then he vamoosed. Sounds to me as much like justifiable homicide as the other killings."

Garcia nodded somberly. "I guess so, knowing Saul Pettit and what would have happened if Gordy had been taken to Lark."

We walked back to the house. I didn't think either Judy or De Bussy had moved from the time we'd left them half an hour before. Judy said, "Now maybe you'll believe me, Sheriff."

"I never doubted you, Mrs. Bishop." Garcia mounted and nodded at De Bussy. "He's not here. Now let her alone. Understand?"

"I understand," De Bussy said.

They turned their horses and rode away. Judy let out a long breath and said, "That's the most horrible man I ever saw, but maybe he got the point and now we'll have some peace."

We did have peace, although it was more on the surface than in Judy's heart. We finished cutting the winter's supply of wood, we dug the vegetables from the garden and stored them in the root cellar, and we drove fifteen head of steers to Stonewall and sold them to the stock buyer who had come out from Trinidad. Then early in November we took two three-year-old fillies to Stonewall and sold them to Olney.

"Now we can slow up," Judy said after we got back. "We've got everything done that has to be done before winter."

We were standing at the corral when she said that. I looked at the great peaks to the west that were now snow-covered. I said, "None too soon, judging from what's happened up there."

"It can happen here any time now," she said. "The way the clouds are moving in, we might get snow tonight."

We walked to the house. I glanced at Judy, thinking these weeks had been hard on her. Every time I had brought the mail, she had glanced through it quickly and then said, "I thought sure I'd hear from Cindy this time."

And I always said in a positive tone, "You'll hear one of these days," and knew I was lying, or at least I wasn't as sure as I pretended to be.

As soon as we walked into the house, I built a fire and Judy started supper. I sat down at the kitchen table and watched her. She had changed since Cindy had left. She wasn't as outgoing, she didn't smile very often, and she talked much less. Sometimes when we were working together, she would go for hours without saying a word. I suspected she was blaming herself for Cindy's leaving. That was wrong, but I didn't know what to say that would give her any comfort.

As we were eating, Judy said, "Well, we've got all the money we're going to make this year. It has to pay the taxes and buy what clothes and groceries we need. Usually I take Cindy and go to Trinidad for several days to buy clothes and stay in a hotel and eat restaurant food, but I won't be doing that this year."

"Another year," I said, and let it go at that.

I had been doing some hard thinking for several days, knowing that the decision I made now would be irrevocable. I had thought back over the years I had worked for the *Rocky Mountain News*, all the time believing I was doing exactly what I wanted to do, but now, after the weeks I had worked for Judy, I knew that my life in Denver was over.

Now I sat with a cup of coffee in front of me just staring at Judy and thinking of all the times I had slept on lumpy mattresses in dirty hotel rooms with bedbugs for company, of the time I had spent in my one-room Denver apartment waiting for my next assignment.

I had wanted excitement, but I'd had enough to last me the rest of my life. I'd wanted travel and I'd had enough of that. If Judy didn't want me for a husband, I would at least go back to Denver, resign my job, wind up my affairs, and look for a job somewhere else. That much of my future I had decided.

I wasn't sure that this was the right time to talk to Judy, but I wasn't sure I would ever find the perfect time. In any case, I had made my decision and there was no sense in staying on if there was no future for me here.

"Judy," I said, "I'm starting to Denver in the morning. I'm going to resign my job. When I was a kid on my parents' ranch, I hated hard work, but I've found out since I came here that it isn't so bad. I'm in better shape now than I've ever been and I feel better. I'd like to stay here and work with you. I've got some savings that I'd invest in the BB if we have any need for it. Maybe we could work out a partnership."

She was watching me intently. Suddenly I realized I was saying it all wrong. When I stopped to get a good breath, she said carefully, "Maybe we could work something out."

"Oh Judy," I said. "There's nothing logical about this and I'm trying so damned hard to be logical. The truth is I love you and I want to marry you. I know I can't take the place of your first husband, but maybe I would have a place of my own. We haven't known each other very long, but the first time I saw you, I had the crazy feeling that we had known each other forever. Anyhow, it's been long enough for me to know I love you and I want to stay here with you."

She smiled again and got up and came around the table to me. She put an arm around me and hugged me. She said, “You don’t know how much good you’ve done me. I couldn’t have managed without you, and I’ve worried about what would happen to me after you leave. I love you and I want to marry you, but I’ve got too many doubts just now about you. After the exciting life you’ve lived, I can’t imagine you being satisfied just staying here. Usually life on the BB is very quiet and dull.”

“Then the answer’s no?”

She began clearing the table. “Oh no, I didn’t say that. I’ve been hoping you would say what you’ve just said, but now that you have said it, I’ve got to live with it for a little while and think about it. I guess Cindy is too much in my mind just now to know what I want for myself. I’ve even thought about selling the ranch and going away.”

“Where?”

“Anywhere.”

She moved to the stove and stood there, her back to me. I got up and went outside, realizing that she had started to cry. It had turned cold and I thought it would be snowing by morning.

I returned to the house in a few minutes and climbed the stairs and went to bed. I lay there for a long time staring at the black ceiling and thinking about the circumstances that had brought me here. I still couldn’t make a solid judgment about Gordy Morgan, but he was beyond doubt the Trouble Kid, trouble to himself and the people who were around him. That much of what the *Tribune* had said about him was true. At least I could thank him for bringing me here and meeting Judy.

At last I dropped off into a fretful sleep. I had a scary dream about being chased by a dozen Hank De Bussys, all of them shooting at me. I woke up shivering and suddenly I was aware that Judy was standing by the window. I sat up, asking, "What's the matter?"

"I couldn't sleep," she said. "You know it's started to snow?"

"I'm not surprised," I said. "Aren't you cold?"

"I'm freezing," she said.

"Come here," I said. "I'll get you warm."

She slipped into bed beside me and I held her in my arms, something I had wanted to do for a long time. After she stopped shivering, I kissed her. I'd wanted to do that, too, for a long time. Suddenly, then, she was alive with a hunger that could not be denied.

CHAPTER XXII

I left in a snowstorm the following morning. Judy had found a sheepskin among her husband's clothes that fitted me, so with the heavy coat and gloves, I didn't get very cold. I couldn't find a hat that fitted me, so I still wore my derby.

I must have made an incongruous figure wearing a suit, a sheepskin coat, and a derby hat that was thrust forward against the wind, my chin tucked close to my chest, but the kind of figure I made was the least of my worries. Fortunately the snow eased off a few miles east of Stonewall and I rode most of the way under a threatening sky.

As soon as I reached Trinidad, I turned my horse in at the livery stable, paid my bill and, going to the depot, bought a round-trip ticket for Denver. I slept part of the way, but mostly I sat half listening to the steady click-click of wheels on rails and worrying about my meeting with the Great Man.

He'd give me hell for being gone so long and not sending in as much copy as he expected, and probably for not trying to follow Gordy. I knew very well that when I told him I was resigning, he would give me an additional dose of fire and brimstone.

I spent most of the following day in my apartment packing everything I wanted to keep in one suitcase and a trunk. I managed to give the rest of it away. I paid my rent that was overdue and told my landlord I was leaving. I drew my money out of the bank and hired a dray to haul my trunk and suitcase to the depot.

For a time I stood looking around my apartment thinking of the years I had called this home, the small amount of time I had actually spent in the apartment, and how little I had accomplished with my life and how little I had saved up for my future years if I couldn't work. Everything I had in a material way was in one suitcase in Trinidad, another suitcase and trunk still in Denver, and the draft that was in my wallet.

The future was something else. The past could not be relived and I was never one to waste my time and energy in regrets. Still, I was struck by the change in my ambitions, the different turn my life had taken in the months since the Great Man had started me on the trail of the elusive Gordy Morgan.

I had hoped to find Gordy and finish my story with a personal touch, my feelings about him when I actually met him face to face. Now I had another one of my hunches that it would never happen. I would probably never see him.

I turned my key over to my landlord and caught a streetcar for downtown. I went directly to the *Rocky Mountain News* office and found Roscoe Gentry still there. I had been concerned about catching him because by now it was late in the afternoon.

For a long time he just sat behind his desk and stared at me, his face getting redder and redder, and then when the pressure became intolerable, he jumped up and bellowed in a voice that could be heard all over the news room, "Where in the God damn hell have you been? I sure made a lousy investment when I sent you on the Gordy

Morgan story. If I'd had an address, I'd have brought you back. I didn't even get a finished story out of it."

"You've got the finish," I said. "He ran off with Judy Bishop's girl and I don't have the foggiest notion where they are." I laid a sheet of paper with a list of my expenses in front of him. "You owe me some back salary. I also ran out of expense money. You owe me $55.62."

"I don't owe you a damned penny," he snapped, his voice barely controlled. "Now I've got another job that's been waiting for you. This time you'd better keep in touch with me. Over in Grand Junction . . ."

"Now wait a minute, Mr. Gentry," I interrupted. "I'm not going to Grand Junction. I am going back to Trinidad. I'm quitting."

He sat down in his chair; or, rather, fell back into it. He stared at me and moistened his lips with the tip of his tongue. "I didn't hear you use the word quit, did I?"

"You did," I said.

"What are you going to do?"

"Work on Mrs. Bishop's ranch," I said, thinking that the less he knew about my plans the better for both of us.

"You are going to work on a ranch?" He sat back and shook his head in disbelief. "Curran, have you gone daft?"

"No, I've finally got my sense back," I said. "If

I have to risk my life to earn a living, it'll be taking a chance on lightning or a bucking horse. I was slugged in a hotel room trying to write your story on Gordy Morgan. I was held by two plug-uglies bigger than me while Saul Pettit knocked hell out of me. I was shot at by two of his cow hands and had to kill one of them to save my life. I was threatened by two of Hank De Bussy's men who would likely have killed me if luck hadn't been running my way. Later on those same men shot up the bunkhouse where I was sleeping." I shook my head. "No, Mr. Gentry, I haven't gone daft. I just want my money."

He leaned forward and scrawled his initials across the bottom of my list of expenses, then he rose. "Get your money from the cashier," he said. "Good luck, Curran. When you get tired of playing cowboy, come back and I'll find something nice and safe for you to do like writing the society page."

He held out his hand and I shook it. I was surprised to see that his eyes were moist. I guess the crusty old bastard did have a human side to him after all. I walked to the door and when I looked back, he was standing behind his desk. I heard him say, "The best investigative reporter I ever had and he wants to be a cowboy."

It was close, but I caught the evening south-bound train. We were late getting into Trinidad, but it was still night. I took a hotel room, thinking there was no sense in looking for Judy at that hour. She had promised to get Mack Olney to do the chores and said she would drive the buckboard into town so we could take my trunk and suitcases home, but I got back to Trinidad a day sooner than I had expected. According to schedule, I could expect her late that afternoon.

I slept a few hours, shaved, and had breakfast, then hunted up a bank and deposited my draft. I didn't know how much cash Judy had on hand, but I knew she had some plans for building up her herd by buying a good whiteface bull and she had told the cattle buyer when he was in Stonewall to keep an eye out for her.

So far she hadn't heard from him and she probably wouldn't until spring. I hadn't seriously talked to her about how much of my money she would need, so the only thing to do was to deposit it and leave it there until we were ready to use it.

For a time I lingered on the street, enjoying the sunshine. The snow had reached this far east and Fisher Peak looked as if it had received a foot or more, but the lower slope above town was almost bare. If there had been any snow here, it was gone. I crossed the brick-paved street to the hotel, deciding there was nothing for me to do all day, so I'd have a drink and after that I'd call on Garcia to see if he had received any word about Gordy and Cindy. Too, I wanted to congratulate him on being re-elected. I had heard about it before I left on my way to Denver.

I stepped into the lobby and there was Judy waiting for me. She rose when she saw me and came to me. She was wearing a dress. I had seldom seen her in one. This was a special dress, a fresh, new dress that was bright blue with a white lace collar and a tight-fitting bodice, a dress that made her look more vibrant and feminine than I had ever seen her before. Still, being male and stupid about such things, it took me a moment to realize she had bought it for me.

She came into my arms and I kissed her, tenderly at first, then with a passion that I knew at once she felt as strongly as I did. For that moment we were alone and the hundreds of people who made up the town of Trinidad did not exist.

When she stepped back, we glanced around and were aware that we were not alone, that the clerk and a drummer and a cleaning woman were all watching us, their amusement plain to read in their faces.

"Never mind them," I said. "I'm glad to see ou and I'm glad to be back."

"I left a day early," she said. "I wanted to do some shopping. I didn't know you were here until I got up this morning and looked at the register."

"Have you had breakfast?" I asked.

"No. I thought I'd look for you first, hoping you were here, and when I found you were, I decided to wait. The clerk said you had left just a minute before I came downstairs. I thought you'd be back soon."

"I've had breakfast," I said, "but I'll have a cup of coffee while you eat."

We turned toward the dining room, glad to get away from the knowing grins that were on the faces of the people in the lobby. We took a table in a back corner. As soon as we were seated, I said, "I like your dress very much."

She blushed, the first time I had seen her blush. She said, "I'm ashamed, Curt, that you have seen me the way you have, wearing a man's clothes and doing a man's work and actually working beside you as if I was a man. If I had known it would turn out this way, I wouldn't have let you do it. Anyhow, I had to buy a dress to show you that I am a woman in spite of the way you have seen me."

I couldn't help smiling. "Judy, Judy," I said, "you have already showed me you are very much a woman."

She tipped her head down and stared at the table top. "I feel guilty about that," she said, then she looked up and added defiantly, "I really was cold."

We both laughed. I said, "It's a new life for both of us. I have officially resigned from the *Rocky Mountain News*."

Her face turned grave. "I've got news. That's why I came a day early. I thought you might get back sooner than you expected and it's important that you hear. I had a letter from Cindy. They're in Durango."

My heart skipped a beat. I sensed what was coming and suddenly I was afraid. This was to be our wedding day and I didn't want anyone or anything to mar it or postpone it, but in that moment I was certain it was going to be postponed.

"Is she all right?" I asked.

"She is except for being frightened," Judy said. "She says Gordy has changed, that he can't face running any more or not knowing when Pettit will catch up with them. She says he's going to commit suicide and if he does, she doesn't want to live. She wants you to come if you are still here. She says there's nobody else she can turn to for help." Judy leaned forward, her hands reaching for mine. "Will you go, Curt?"

"Of course," I said.

So I was not finished with Gordy Morgan after all. I wondered, too, where the idea came from that a man was master of his destiny.

CHAPTER XXIII

The snow had been very heavy on the passes and the train was slowed up so it took me a day and a half to reach Durango, thirty-six hours that gave me plenty of time to think. I was amazed that Cindy had called on me for help. When we had been together on the BB, she had kept her distance. I didn't think she disliked me, but, rather, it had been the fact that I wanted to see Gordy, and that he refused to see me—so she probably felt I blamed her.

As I thought back over those days, I realized I had pressed her, trying to persuade her that it was best for Gordy to see me, but I wasn't sure I had convinced her. Gordy was like a wild animal who was afraid of being caged and perhaps Cindy shared that fear. Still, thinking back, I wasn't at all sure I could have helped Gordy if he had been willing to see me. All I could have done was to have rounded out my story and Gordy didn't give a damn about that.

What could I do for either one of them now? I didn't have any idea and I didn't know what Cindy expected of me or even why she had sent for me. I had reached the point where I didn't really care much either way about Gordy. In a way he had made his own bed. I felt that taking Cindy with him and making her share his life as a fugitive was unforgivable.

In any case, if Gordy wanted to commit suicide, I couldn't stop him. I wouldn't have come if Judy hadn't asked me. It would have doomed our marriage from the first if I had refused. My sole responsibility was to Cindy. Somehow I had to talk her into going back with me regardless of what happened to Gordy.

Cindy had written that I was to stay in the Strater Hotel. She would check every morning to see if I had arrived. I stepped off the train in Durango into a good six inches of snow. The sky had cleared and the sun was dazzling on the new snow. The Strater was only about two blocks from the depot. I don't know what the temperature was, but it was cold, and I was glad to reach the warm comfort of the lobby.

I registered and was given the key to a room on the second floor. I laid my suitcase on the bed and took time to shave, then went downstairs for breakfast. When I finished, I looked around the lobby for Cindy, but she wasn't in sight.

She hadn't said what time she would be here, so I had no reason to worry, but I was jumpy and began to wonder if something had happened to her. Maybe Gordy had taken off again and Cindy had gone with him. If that had happened, I would be helpless. I had no idea where they would go or even where they had been staying, and yet I knew I could not go back to Judy and say I had lost them.

I don't really know why my nerves were drawn as tight as they were. I seldom worried about the what ifs and the might have beens and the things that could happen, but I couldn't dispel a gloomy sense of disaster. Perhaps that was the reason I reacted the way I did when I stepped into the bar and saw Saul Pettit.

Of all the men in the world, Pettit was the last one I expected to see in Durango. De Bussy's men must have tracked Gordy here and sent word to Pettit. He was standing at the bar, his back to me. He was alone.

I guess I stood motionless for several seconds as surprise gave way to a cold, murderous fury. In that instant I could think of nothing except the two toughs holding me while Pettit drove his fist into my belly.

I walked up to him and grabbed him by a shoulder and hauled him around to face me and then I hit him on the chin. It was the best blow I ever struck and it gave me more pleasure than any other. He went back and down, his arms flung upward in the air. I had the distinct pleasure of hearing his head hit the floor with a very solid crack.

"You son of a bitch," I said. "How does it feel when you don't have a couple of your hardcases holding my hands behind my back while you give me a beating?"

The bartender yelled at someone to call the police, but I didn't look back at him. Pettit lay where he fell, one hand coming up to feel of his jaw. He was wearing a gun, and I expected him to get up and try for it, but he didn't. He just lay there, not saying a word.

"Get up," I said. "You've got a gun. Use it if you don't want to try your fists."

He still didn't move and he didn't speak. He just stared at me with a violence of hatred I had never seen before in a man's eyes. I don't know how long I stood there staring down at him, but suddenly I remembered Cindy and why I had come to Durango. The last thing I wanted was to be arrested for assault and thrown into jail. I turned and strode out, realizing belatedly that I had done a very stupid thing.

Cindy was in the lobby. When she saw me, she cried, "Curt," and ran to me and threw her arms around me. "I knew you'd come. I knew it."

I hugged her, surprised at the warmth of her greeting because our relationship as I have said had been strictly hands off. I said, "Let's go upstairs to my room where we can talk."

She nodded and we turned to the stairs and climbed them, one of her hands tucked under my arm. I wanted to get out of the lobby so that if the police did come, they wouldn't see me. If they couldn't find me, I thought the chances were good they'd forget the whole thing.

Unlocking the door, I motioned for Cindy to sit in the one chair that was in the room and I dropped onto the bed. My anger had cooled and now I felt uneasy with the knowledge that I had lost my temper and acted without the least bit of logic, a dangerous thing to do in view of my reason for coming to Durango.

"All right," I said. "Let's hear about this business of Gordy committing suicide."

"In a way I lied in my letter," she said. "It isn't that he'll shoot himself or anything like that. It's just that he won't run away any more. All this time he's been afraid that Pettit would find him and kill him without giving him a chance. He says he can't stand the suspense of not knowing from one minute to the next whether Pettit is out there waiting for him."

"He doesn't need to worry about committing suicide," I said. "Pettit will take care of it for him."

"I know," she said. "That's why I said in the letter he's determined to commit suicide. Bringing Pettit here is committing suicide just the same as if he shoots himself."

I got up and walked to the window and looked down into the street. I asked, "What do you mean, bringing Pettit here?"

"He wrote to Pettit and told him where he was," Cindy said. "He told me he had to end it one way or another and he'd rather be dead than go on like this. He said if he went back to Lark now, he knew he'd be killed, so he thought that if he could get Pettit out here, he'd have a chance. He wrote to Pettit that he wanted to talk and maybe they could reach a settlement. He said he had a good ranch at Lark and if he could work something out with Pettit, we'd go back there and live."

It was a wild idea and he must have known it. Pettit wouldn't talk. The only way he would settle their trouble was to kill Gordy. I thought this over, but I couldn't get a handle on it. Gordy was too smart to think he could arrive at any kind of a truce with talk.

"I don't get it, Cindy," I said finally. "Gordy ought to know how it will end."

"I think he's a little crazy," she said, "but I can understand why he would be. He's changed since we left home. He's more nervous. Jumps at every noise. He's on guard all the time. He wrote to Pettit telling him where we lived and to come alone for the talk. I think he meant it when he said he'd rather die than live the way we've been living." She paused, then added bitterly. "Living this way has made me a little crazy, too, Curt. Or maybe it's the injustice of it. Gordy isn't to blame for what happened."

I looked at her for a moment, thinking that people do go crazy when hard pressure has been on them long enough. Cindy was thinner than she had been when she'd left the BB. She had always been very neat, but now her dress was torn and dirty, and her hair wasn't pinned up as carefully as it used to be. Now it hung down her back in a dark mass that looked as if it hadn't been brushed for days.

"I guess we're all a little crazy if you want to put it that way," I said, "or this kind of situation wouldn't have come about." I hesitated, not wanting to hurt her, but the idea that I could do anything at this point got under my hide. I asked, "What do you think I can do?"

"You kept telling me when I was home that it would be best for Gordy if he talked to you, that you could do something for him."

I couldn't bring myself to tell her that I didn't work for the *Rocky Mountain News* any longer. I stood with my back to her, my gaze on the street. I said, "You think Gordy will talk to me now?"

"Yes," she said. "I told him he had to. I said that if he didn't, I'd go back home with you. You told me the law didn't want him."

"It still doesn't as far as I know," I said. "Garcia has been re-elected so that isn't likely to change, but I can't keep Pettit off his back."

"I know that," she said, "but you used to say that if he went to the sheriff and asked for protection . . ."

"I can tell him that," I interrupted, "and I think Garcia would try. The trouble is I'm not sure if his protection would be adequate. Anyhow, if Gordy is hellbent on talking to Pettit, he won't listen to any advice I can give him."

"Pettit won't be here for another day or two," she said. "If I have figured the time . . ."

I turned to face her. "He's already here, Cindy."

She froze, her hands forming tight little fists

on her lap. Her face drained of color. She whispered, "How do you know that?"

"I saw him," I answered. "I had a tussle with him in the bar just before you got here."

"Oh, my God," she said. "I was so sure you could get here ahead of him. Come on. He's in strange country. It'll take him some time to find the cabin. Maybe we can beat him."

"You expect me to ride double?" I asked. "Or are we getting a horse from a livery stable?"

"I brought Gordy's bay for you," she said. "Come on."

She opened the door and went flying down the stairs. I followed, but not with any hope of success. I had come this far. I had to see it through to the finish, but I sensed that I had a front seat to a tragedy.

CHAPTER XXIV

Two horses were tied at the hitch rack in front of the hotel, the sorrel Cindy had brought from her home and a bay with white stockings and a star in his forehead, Gordy's horse that I had heard about in Lark. We mounted and took a road up the east side of the Animas River.

One thing bothered me. It wasn't like Pettit to be here by himself. Of course he hadn't expected to see me in the hotel bar, and he could logically expect Gordy to stay out of Durango, but for him to tackle Gordy by himself, if my judgment of the man was correct, did not add up. I remembered him saying that he was going to kill Gordy personally, but still it was his way to give himself some insurance, either a couple of his cow hands, or De Bussy and at least one of his men.

The question obviously had not occurred to Cindy. I knew she wasn't of a mind to listen just then, but I found myself watching both sides of the road and the thick patch of timber along the river. This had all the earmarks of an ambush, although I saw no reason why Cindy and I should be targets, certainly not until Pettit's debt to Gordy had been paid. Still, I was jumpy as my gaze kept whipping back and forth from one side of the road to the other.

The snow was not deep enough to slow us up significantly. By the time we had traveled a mile or more I began to wonder if we'd catch up with Pettit. Or was he still behind us in Durango? If the latter were the case, we'd have a chance to talk to Gordy and try to dissuade him from meeting Pettit. On the other hand, if Pettit was ahead of us, the fat was in the fire and there wasn't anything we could do.

Another half mile, then we rounded a curve in the road and I saw Pettit ahead of us, so I had the answer to my question. He was walking his horse as if he was in no hurry. Maybe he wanted Gordy to see him and thought this slow approach would not alarm the boy. Cindy apparently had not seen him, or if she had, she likely did not realize who he was.

"How much farther?" I asked.

"We're there."

She pointed to a log cabin set near the edge of the cottonwoods that lined the river bank. Just as she spoke, Pettit reined up and called out to Gordy. We had lost our bet.

I called, "Pull up, Cindy. That's Pettit ahead of us."

"No," she yelled back as she raced on ahead of me. "We've got to stop them some way."

It was too late, but Cindy put her sorrel into a run and I couldn't let her go on alone. I thought that at this point it wasn't right for us to interfere with Gordy's scheme, whatever it was, but there was no arguing with Cindy. I simply had no choice.

Any qualms I had about interfering was wasted effort because the final act of the tragedy was played out before us in the next few seconds. Before we were close enough to do anything, a bearded man stepped out of the cabin, paused to unbuckle his gun belt and let it drop, then rammed his hands into his pockets as a kid might and walked toward Pettit, swaggering in the way a show-off kid would do, and that, I sensed, was exactly what he wanted Pettit to think he was. Maybe that was the way he had been when the cow man knew him.

Gordy said something, but we were too far away to hear what it was, then Pettit said something, or I thought he did. He was leaning forward motioning with one hand and probably cursing or goading Gordy, or both.

Suddenly Gordy jerked his hands out of his pocket and raised his right arm. I heard the shot, I saw the puff of smoke, and I saw Saul Pettit slump forward over the horn. Just as he fell out of his saddle, rifles cracked from the timber and Gordy was slammed against the wall of his cabin. His feet went out from under him and sprawled on the ground a few feet from Pettit.

Cindy screamed but she never slowed up. A moment later we reached the fallen men. Pettit's horse had whirled and galloped away. Cindy reached Gordy ahead of me and dismounted and knelt beside him. Whoever had shot Gordy could have knocked us off like a pair of ducks. I expected it to happen, but as I swung to the ground, I saw two men ride out of the timber downstream from the cabin and, putting their horses into a dead run, headed south toward Durango. I wasn't sure, but in that one quick glance I gave them, I thought I recognized Hank De Bussy and Jerry Hahn.

I knelt in the snow on one side of Gordy

opposite Cindy. She was crying and holding his hands and telling me to go for a doctor. He was alive, but no doctor could have helped Gordy Morgan. He had been hit both in the chest and in the belly, and I guessed he didn't have more than a minute of life left in him.

His eyes flickered open. He whispered, "Cindy, I didn't think it would end this way. I thought I could handle him. I . . . wanted . . . to . . . live . . . I . . ."

Blood bubbled at the corners of his mouth. He took one long shuddering breath and was gone. I rose, thankful to be alive, and knelt beside Pettit. He was dead, a round hole in his forehead. Gordy's derringer was half buried in the snow between the two bodies.

Cindy leaned down and kissed Gordy on the lips. When she rose, his blood had made a scarlet smear on her lips.

She looked at me and whispered, "We couldn't keep it from happening, could we?"

"No," I said. "It wouldn't have made any difference anyway. I don't think he would have let us stop it. He had to play it out to the end."

There was no way to be sure exactly what he'd had in mind, but it had been impractical and naive whatever it was. He should have known that Saul Pettit was always a man to play it safe and hedge his bet some way.

I'm guessing, but I think Pettit wanted to gloat

and punish Gordy with his mouth before he killed him, that De Bussy and Hahn had been ordered to keep their guns on Gordy and fire if he made a hostile move. They must have been fooled when he dropped his gun belt. They probably fired the instant he lifted his arm, but they were too late by a split second, a very small interval of time that spelled death for Saul Pettit.

I wasn't sure what Pettit's plan had been, either. Maybe he planned to take the boy back to Lark, although he'd said he wanted to personally kill Gordy and he could have done it here as well as in Lark. More likely, he wanted to take him farther from town, perhaps back into the mountains before he killed him and could hide his body. Or he may only have wanted to gloat for a moment and then intended to draw his gun and shoot Gordy in cold blood.

Whatever his plan, if Cindy and I had been in the cabin and he had known it, he would have tried to kill us. If Cindy had been alone, he would certainly have succeeded.

I looked at Cindy, who was standing over Gordy's body and staring down at his bearded, old-young face as if she still could not believe it had happened.

I said, "I'll get Pettit's horse."

We took the bodies into Durango, with Cindy riding behind me on her sorrel. We turned the bodies over to the sheriff and told him what had happened. I said I thought De Bussy and Hahn had killed Gordy. The sheriff promised to keep his eyes open for them, but I was convinced that he had no intention of seriously looking for them.

We returned to the cabin and Cindy gathered up a few things she wanted to keep, including the gold Gordy had left. It wasn't much, less than one hundred dollars. She gave it to me to keep for her, saying that it wouldn't have lasted much longer. Gordy hadn't wanted to go to work because he would have had to show himself and he was afraid to do that as long as Pettit was alive.

"He knew we couldn't live much longer the way we had been living," she said in a low tone. "He was certain that Pettit's men were looking for him, so he didn't want anyone to see him. He kept gunnysacks over the windows. I was the one who went to town for food. Twice someone knocked on the door and he wouldn't let me open it. Once I peeked through one of the windows and saw two men. When we didn't open the door, they got on their horses and rode away, but Gordy said they were probably watching the cabin."

"We know one thing," I said. "Committing suicide was not his intention."

"No," she said, "but that is the way it turned out."

I wondered if De Bussy and Hahn had somehow tracked Gordy here and had guessed he was holed up somewhere near Durango. Maybe they had seen Cindy leave the cabin, although I didn't know how they could have recognized her. Or again, they might have found Gordy's bay in the shed. They would, of course, have had a description of the horse. In any case, it was immaterial since Gordy had written to Pettit and it was his letter which had precipitated the final act of the tragedy.

We buried Gordy the next day on a wind-swept hillside, snowflakes swirling through the air, and that afternoon we boarded a train for Trinidad. Cindy had said almost nothing from the time we had left the cabin the day before. The tears had dried up, but her stony face told me her grief was piling up inside and it would be a long time before she felt at peace with herself.

We were silent for a long time. We sat listening to the whistle of the locomotive ahead of us, saw the black clouds of smoke swirl past us along our windows, and we felt the coach sway as the train gathered speed.

I had put off telling her about Judy and me, but I knew I had to do it and this was as good a time as any. I said, "I ought to tell you, Cindy, that your mother and I will be married as soon as you and I get back."

She tried to smile, one hand moving to hold my hand that was closer to her. She said, "I'm glad,

Curt. I'm not surprised. I saw it in both of you almost as soon as you came."

"I hope I can be a substitute father for you," I said. "I know I can't replace your own father, but if you'll accept me, I'll . . ."

"I couldn't have if you hadn't come when I needed you," she interrupted, "but now I can." She swallowed and looked down at her lap. "I'm carrying Gordy's baby and I'm not ashamed. We were never married. We kept talking about it, but once we got to the cabin, he wouldn't leave." She looked up at me. "What will mama say?"

"She will love you just the same," I said. "She never stopped loving you. All she wants is for you to be home."

She started to cry again, the first time that I knew about in more than twenty-four hours. I put an arm around her and she collapsed against my shoulder as if all of her strength had gone out of her and she needed me to hold her.

My thoughts turned to Gordy Morgan, of how some people in Lark who had known him all his life considered him a wonderful and fine young man almost without fault, and yet Jonathan Aldridge had said he'd had them, that he would have got Cissy Edwards into his bed if he could and now he had got Cindy pregnant but had never married her.

I thought of what the Trinidad *Tribune* had said

about him, of Pettit who had considered him a vicious killer and an outlaw. Was he good? Or bad? A saint or a devil? I still, after all this time, did not know the truth about the boy, but, like Pilate, I could well ask what was truth.

For that matter, what was truth about me, or Judy, or Cindy? What is truth about any man or woman? We are told in the Bible not to judge, yet every one of us judges each day of our lives. The law judges; and justice, as man tries to mete it out to his fellow men, is a touchy and questionable matter about which we more often than not do not agree. I knew then I would never write the end of the Gordy Morgan story for Roscoe Gentry. He could read about Gordy's killing in a Durango news release.

I looked down at Cindy and saw that she was asleep, and that, as with her tears, might have been the first time in twenty-four hours. She was going to need all of the love that Judy and I could give her, and perhaps our love, with the help of time, could heal her wounds.

Wayne D. Overholser has won three Golden Spur awards from the Western Writers of America and has a long list of fine Western titles to his credit. He was born in Pomeroy, Washington, and attended the University of Montana, University of Oregon, and the University of Southern California before becoming a public school teacher and principal in various Oregon communities. He began writing for Western pulp magazines in 1936 and within a couple of years was a regular contributor to Street & Smith's *Western Story* and Fiction House's *Lariat Story Magazine. Buckaroo's Code* (1948) was his first Western novel and remains one of his best. In the 1950s and 1960s, having retired from academic work to concentrate on writing, he would publish as many as four books a year under his own name or a pseudonym, most prominently as Joseph Wayne. *The Bitter Night*, *The Lone Deputy*, and *The Violent Land* are among the finest of the early Overholser titles. He was asked by William MacLeod Raine, that dean among Western writers, to complete his last novel after Raine's death. Some of Overholser's most rewarding novels were actually collaborations with other Western writers: *Colorado Gold* with Chad Merriman and *Showdown at Stony Creek* with Lewis B. Patten. Overholser's Western novels, no matter under what name they have been published, are based on a solid knowledge of the history and customs of the American frontier West, particularly when set in his two favorite Western states, Oregon and Colorado. When it comes to his characters, he writes with skill, an uncommon sensitivity, and a consistently vivid and accurate vision of a way of life unique in human history.

Center Point Large Print
600 Brooks Road / PO Box 1
Thorndike, ME 04986-0001 USA

(207) 568-3717

US & Canada:
1 800 929-9108
www.centerpointlargeprint.com